In a few decades, medical progress will make it possible to extend human life significantly, even to infinity. How would this change people's minds, actions and coexistence? These are the questions the four stories deal with. DURATION – as the new process is called by the author – plays a decisive role in all of them.

Their styles are rather different, including realistic storytelling, science fiction, crime thriller and a philosophically inspired grotesque.

A LITTLE MORE TIME: Irmgard Rominski receives an offer to be the first one with a significantly prolonged lifespan.

GAMMA FLASH: The spaceship "Golden promise" is en route to the Alpha Centauri star system.

BOMB DEPOSIT: Sirlana's self-driving car is hacked and hijacked.

ZEUS IS TELLING A JOKE: The "immortal gods" are wasting away because no one believes in them.

Peter Werner Richter, born in 1946, grew up in Freiburg, Germany. He studied economics and regional planning. After the fall of the Berlin Wall, he moved to Eastern Germany, where he worked as a town planner. This job, which often bears the traits of a real-life satire, certainly inspired him to realise his secretly harboured literary ambitions. His professional experiences are probably responsible for the fact that his primary interests lie in foreseeable developments in the near future.

Today, P.W. Richter lives in a small village in the state of Brandenburg, Germany and devotes himself entirely to writing.

A Little More Time

Four Stories about Eternal Life

Produced and published by: BoD – Books on Demand, Norderstedt
Hamburg 2023

First published in Germany by BOD, with the title
Zeus erzählt einen Witz,
Hamburg 2016

ISBN: 9783757823801

Content

Just when you are ready to start,
you have to die.

Immanuel Kant
1724 – 1804

I

A Little More Time

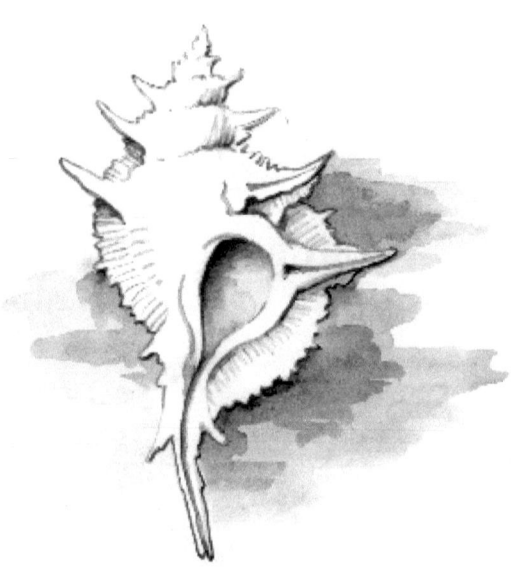

The car arrived a little earlier than announced. Even much sooner would have been fine for Irmgard Rominski. She had been waiting at the window for more than an hour, dressed in her coat and hat. A few days ago she'd received an announcement she would be picked up at ten a.m. in front of her house, and since then she had hardly managed to get anything done. When the car finally found a parking space, she was already in the street, and the driver hurried to open the door and help her in.

With a quick look in the back of the Mercedes, he made sure the old lady was secured and sitting comfortably. Then he steered the car out of the parking space, drove trough the bumpy lanes of the southern suburbs of Eberswalde, and finally turned left onto the 167, which led straight to the motorway.

The man drove calmly and with concentration, like someone who had been doing his job for many years. Irmgard Rominski estimated him to be in his late forties.

'Where are you taking me?' she asked.

'To Berlin, to the Charité.'

'I know that. I mean, where exactly?'

'To the *Campus Mitte*. That's near the *Reichstag*.'

Irmgard wondered if he didn't want to tell her the exact destination, or if he couldn't because he didn't remember the name of the institute. To him, it probably sounded as curious as hundreds of other scientific institutions. She decided on the latter.

'Is it perhaps the Institute for Cell- and Neurobiology?' she asked.

'That's right, ma'am, that's the name. You are expected there at eleven thirty.'

She nodded. Of course, she knew the time and place; it had been mentioned in the invitation. But it reassured her to hear it again.

The car drove silently; it had an electric engine like most newer vehicles. Outside the old buildings of the Crane Construction Company passed by, like in a film. But the car's slight sway, caused by the poor condition of the road, made it clear that it was she who was moving.

Irmgard felt the tension of the last days slowly easing. Now a first step has been taken, she thought. Now things are on the move. The fact that she still had to make a serious decision seemed only a formality.

She knew the Institute for Cell- and Neurobiology well. As a professor of evolutionary biology at Humboldt University, she had often attended lectures in other fields to keep up with the latest findings. Some years ago, the institute had made a real splash with its breakthroughs in stem cell research. It attracted worldwide attention, especially with its new approaches to treating the widespread Alzheimer's Disease. Though Alzheimer's was not her field of expertise and did not affect her personally, despite her seventy years, the research on it was of such general importance that one should always stay best-informed. Well, while it lasts, she thought.

'We're almost on the motorway,' the driver said, as they followed the elegant sweep of the road over the tree-lined Finow Canal and entered the next village. The buildings stood closer to the roadway here, and the car slowed its pace. It seemed to her they were only rolling at walking speed through the hotch-potch of small houses, some of which dated from the GDR Era and some from before. The colourful shrubs and trees in the tiny front gardens scarcely softened the drabness of the unadorned façades.

'A bypass would be fine here,' the driver remarked, obviously trying to make a little small talk.

'Yes, they've been planning it for about forty years now,' Irmgard answered.

'Oh! And still not finished?'

'No. It will probably take another forty years before it's ready!'

'I don't think we'll live to see that.'

She sighed. You might, she thought. I might not.

Big blue signposts arose in front of them, and when they had passed the slip road, the grey ribbon of the motorway lay before them, straight and long like the downhill slope of a ski jump, leading directly to the Charité Anatomical Centre in the heart of Berlin. The electric engine accelerated silently but powerfully, pressing Irmgard into the upholstery.

What am I getting into, she thought. Looking back, she realised the first omen had already occurred on her seventieth birthday, just four weeks ago. Among the gratulants was a guest she had never met before.

On that special day in 2033, the sun had summoned up all its strength to create a summer's day in late September, which allowed the celebration to be held in the garden behind the house. For a few days, her two daughters had forgotten their eternal quarrels and managed the entire organisation on their own. That is to say, lending a hand almost everywhere and kindly but firmly ordering their mother out of the kitchen and the rooms to be decorated. Even their husbands had appeared for a short time and taken care of the technical installations. Irmgard had not taken all this for granted, and appreciated it as a special expression of family harmony.

Finally, on the day of the celebration, almost twenty people were gathered in the garden, the inner circle of her family. She was happy, except for those moments when she thought of Thomas, her husband. He was no longer with her. He had died two years ago 'after a long and serious illness'', the usual euphemism for 'cancer''. In his case, it had applied in a terrible way.

Then there were some unexpected guests who were welcomed with a big hello by the others. She had not invited them but was still happy about their visit. One of them was the editor of the local newspaper, whom she already knew from previous interviews. And there was a delegation of colleagues from Humboldt University. Even the dean of her faculty had turned up and congratulated her personally. With a theatrical gesture, he handed her a large flat package, which, as she correctly suspected, contained the latest illustrated book on Humboldt University history. An ordinary standard edition, initially intended as a present for the university's honourable guests from abroad, but more often used as a makeshift gift for all occasions.

But this package was no ordinary gift, for on its cover was attached a whimsical whitish shape. It was about twenty centimetres high and had long appendages that could almost be called spikes. They were decorated with numerous red bows, which gave the whole thing a carnivalesque appearance. It painfully confirmed Irmgard's estimate of her colleagues' aesthetic taste. But the mere idea of presenting her with this sculpture, using the university as its base, so to speak, she found quite impressive.

It was the shell of a sea snail, a Siratus alabaster. one could find it kitschy or mysterious – it was clear to everyone that this thing must have a deeper meaning.

The alabaster snail belongs to the family of spiny snails. It consists almost more of spines than shell, which is actually more of a hindrance for snails that crawl glidingly – in this case with predatory intent – because they could easily get stuck. So why aren't these animals content with a simple shell, like their relatives, the famous cowries, for example? Not to mention the marine nudibranches, which, as the name suggests, do not have a shell at all.

The question had suddenly occurred to her during a discussion on evolutionary mechanisms. It had not left her since. A student of hers claimed the spines were meant as a defence against other carnivores. 'Yes, perhaps,' she had replied. 'But that is certainly not the whole truth.'

All her scientific work since then had revolved around this question: How could it be that some living beings carried around a jumble of body parts, obviously of little use but needed a large amount of nutrients and energy and could even put their owners in great danger? Were we humans simply too stupid to see the point?

4

No, she'd said. There *is* no sense. It is pretty clear that even 'senseless' features are not necessarily eliminated by nature, as long as they do not have a detrimental effect on the daily struggle for survival. This, however, is what happened to the giant deer Megaloceros, a contemporary of the mammoth and the woolly rhinoceros. Like its modern successors, this stag grew new antlers every year. But unlike them, they covered a span of up to *four metres*! He didn't have them because he needed them – he had them because he could afford them. To show off, so to speak.

At this point in her lectures, she never forgot to compare it to the drivers of big, expensive posh cars, which always led to great hilarity in the hall. The megaloceros's luck, however, ran out when the last ice age glaciers retreated northward. The forests became denser again, and the trees refused to leave distances of four metres between their trunks. Noble cars and spiny snails would suffer a similar fate as soon as their biotopes became too cramped. *So in nature,* she concluded, *everything not forbidden is allowed.*

A nice sentence that the students were happy to take with them as general wisdom. As she pointed out, it also applied to life in a much deeper sense. Natural life itself seemed as superfluous on the planet as the spines of the alabaster snail or the antlers of the deer. Life only existed because inanimate matter could not prevent it, apart from the fact that it could not even intend to.

The memories of her scientific activities warmed her heart. The driver, who regularly glanced in the mirror to see if his passenger was comfortable, did not miss her pensive smile.

'Is it a pleasant visit you are making?' he asked.

Her cheerful mood puzzled him, for most elderly people came to the Charité for medical treatment, not for a pleasant occasion. And these persons came with their own means or were brought by ambulance, not by a service car with a driver, and not over such a large distance. This Irmgard Rominski seemed to him quite spry, as they used to say about elderly people. He had noticed that right away, as he'd seen her rushing towards his car in Eberswalde. So she was probably not a case for the hospital. But that she was going to an official appointment also seemed unlikely to him. None of his passengers smiled when he drove them to an appointment.

'I don't know yet.' Her smile disappeared and gave way to a thoughtful expression. 'That depends on what they're going to tell me.' The driver seemed a little too curious to her. She didn't feel like explaining the whole issue to him, also because he probably wouldn't have understood. Or would he? She faltered. Perhaps he of all people?

There was also a person in the university delegation she had never seen before. A petite man of around fifty, dressed just as casually as the other guests, with Asian features and a reserved demeanour. He was introduced to Irmgard as Professor Yi from Seoul, who had held a chair at the Charité for several years. Despite her good contacts to the university hospital, this had escaped her attention, but at least she thought she could vaguely remember some articles under the name Yi. The customary small talk with him was not difficult for her, as the media were full of reports and speculations about Korea these days.

'Do you think your two parts of the country will come together in the near future?' she asked.

After all, the North had been moving discretely towards the South in recent years, reacting quite calmly to the latter's military manoeuvres – that is, not threatening with World War III on any occasion – and even relaxing the censorship a little. The Western media had made this a focal topic during the previous summer slump; since then, the word *reunification* had dominated the headlines.

'Well, the beginning is half the way,' Yi answered ambiguously. 'We have learnt a lot from Germany,' he added with a smile.

'I hope you will use our example to do better.'

'Oh, the Koreans think you've done very well. And you did it fast! That is very important!'

'First of all, we unified the German bureaucracy! Hopefully, they'll take a more generous view of that in Korea.'

'Oh, I'm afraid not.'

They smiled, and after a slight bow he disappeared to join the groups at the back of the garden.

Irmgard Rominski couldn't shake off the feeling that he was still secretly watching her.

A second conversation took place in the late afternoon. Yi sat down next to her at the garden table with a glass of mineral water. He said abruptly, 'I have read your book on the control mechanisms of evolution. It is highly interesting, I must say.'

She felt a little taken off guard. 'I see the Koreans flatter just as boldly as the Germans,' she said.

'No, seriously. I think you are consistently carrying forward Darwin's ideas. The theses on selection-free mutation, for example, are also discussed in our country. You should definitely give your lectures in Seoul too, we would be very pleased...'

Irmgard looked him in the eyes, which were smiling mischievously behind his glasses. You could almost believe him, she thought. 'Oh, you know,' she murmured thoughtfully, 'Korea... isn't that more or less on the other side of the world?'

'Not quite. But if you would like to, we would of course be happy to support you as part of our cooperation with New Zealand as well. So, if you mean to...'

'Oh, stop it, Mr Yi, I'm an old woman! Just turned seventy. Seventy! I don't like travelling anymore. I'm wobbly on my feet and not quite right in my head!'

'No, Mrs Rominski, you are young, believe me!' Again, he beamed at her like a schoolboy. 'You are really young. I can see it!'

With that he had managed to make her feel exactly as she had just stated, wobbly on her feet and confused in the head. She was usually good with compliments on her health and appearance, but with this fifty-year-old Mr Yi, it was something else. Something she couldn't fathom.

'I still have a question.' Now he sounded completely matter-of-fact again. 'A question about your field of expertise. May I?'

7

'Very well. If you stick to the facts, ask.'

'I'm thinking of symbioses, for example. What do you think, can mutation and selection really explain these special adaptations of individual organisms that we find everywhere? The ones that look like both sides know each other intimately and evolve towards each other?'

She looked at him warily from the side. Was he serious, or starting to flirt again? 'Are you a creationist?' she asked gruffly.

'I just mean – that question does arise. Wouldn't this be the next chapter in your research, so to speak?'

She turned her face away. His profound smile, that infinite confidence in his gaze… they would have completely upset her. Of course, he had hit her right on the nerve. Was it so obvious what she secretly dreamt about in her quiet hours? Was he perhaps one of those all-knowing symbionts he had just spoken of? She felt the urge to get up and check what was happening in the kitchen, but stayed put.

'You know, it's my research, but it's open to everyone. Not only is it open to anyone to read, it's open to carry it on. And there are many young scientists who can earn their spurs here. And are already doing so.' She took a sip of her drink. 'You have to know when to let go. Truly, things are no longer down to me.'

Yi objected. 'Things are down to everyone! Isn't that what you say here, in Berlin?'

*

A week later, the message came that was to shake her life from the ground up. It was not an e-mail but a real letter on paper. And it had not been delivered by the post office but by a special messenger, who had only handed the letter over on presentation of the recipient's ID and signature. The sender was the Institute for Cell- and Neurobiology in Berlin. When she tore the envelope open, her vague assumption that it was a letter from Professor Yi was confirmed. He wrote:

8

Dear Mrs Rominski,

I would like to congratulate you once again on your very successful birthday party. I also want to thank you for welcoming an uninvited guest so kindly. I may state that I was deeply impressed by our conversation in your garden.

You said that you have to let go of your place in research. I got the impression that you said this out of respect and humility for nature, which has brought us forth and thus also has the right to take us back. You are honoured by this attitude. I hope you will not blame me if I nevertheless believe that this is not the whole truth. Our conversation showed me that you would very much like to continue working if you were offered the appropriate perspective.

I am honoured to be able to inform you that our institute can now offer you this perspective.

Please treat the following with utmost discretion...

Irmgard Rominski stopped reading and let the letter sink. She was still standing next to the entrance door of her large house, staring into the wardrobe mirror without seeing herself. Who was this mysterious Professor Yi? While her thoughts wandered to the situation in the garden, she felt a slight dizziness and hurried to get into the living room, where she let herself sink into an armchair. From the start, she had suspected that something was wrong with this person! Looking back, it seemed to her that his friendliness – one could even speak of a certain charm – had also something intrusive about it, something illicitly confidential, especially considering he had come to her party as a stranger. She wanted to kick herself for not becoming suspicious...

Who could have guessed that at her party, which she wanted to enjoy, where she wanted to feel really good once more in the company of her loved ones and friends (because who knew what was to come at her advanced age?)... that such a dubious well-wisher as this Yi would turn up? He had checked her out and, at the same time, softened her up like an insurance agent. But perhaps she was focusing too much on the dark side. She hadn't even finished reading the letter. She adjusted her glasses and picked it up again.

For over a decade, our institute has been researching the possibility of prolonging the human lifespan. We have not gone public with this because it is a highly sensitive development that could be dangerously abused in the hands of malevolent interest groups. The criminal machinations in the trade of human organs are a well known and very sad example.

You will be pleased to learn that our Berlin institute, in cooperation with the Clinical Research Institute of the SNUH, Seoul, made a breakthrough in the intended direction several years ago. We have already tested the method (Anti Ageing Approach – AAA) in laboratory experiments. All experiments have resulted in a significant increase in the average lifespan of the test animals.

SNUH, she thought. Seoul National University. And what did the 'H" stand for? Hospital, perhaps? Then it would be an organisation similar to the Charité. She found it very gratifying how globally connected the local institutes were. For no rational reason, she saw this Yi in a more favourable light again. Perhaps her confusion was only based on the slight differences in behaviour.

The final experiment with primates has also been extremely successful so far. Please understand that these experiments can only be finally evaluated when the primates die. At present, it does not look like this will happen soon. Not only are they in good health, there are also clear signs of rejuvenation.

We are sure that AAA is now ready for use in human medicine. Naturally, it is not yet an approved treatment. However, our cooperation partners believe that a selected group of people should already benefit from the advantages of our findings.

I like to recall our conversation at your party. There I gained the impression – no, I am quite sure – that your spiritual aspiration is also directed towards our mutual goal, the

improvement of human life. I would like to ask you to con-
tinue on this path! Give your plans a little more time! I take
the liberty of quoting from your writings: What nature does
not strictly forbid is permitted!

You sly fox! Trying to defeat me at my own game! Attempts like that, she thought, always fail. At least with me. Nobody likes to be beaten with his own words. And besides, he argues in a very suggestive way. What does it mean – our mutual goal of improving human life? That sounds almost as respectable as the claims of the agricultural genetic engineering industry to fight world hunger.

> *Using AAA would probably extend your life expectancy by twenty to thirty years. Enough time to see all your wishes and plans come true.*
>
> *I'm sure you have questions. We can discuss all this on site at the Charité. I have reserved a ride for you in a week's time. Our driver will contact you by phone beforehand.*
>
> *Thank you again for your understanding and discretion!*
> *Yours sincerely*
> *Prof. Dr. Yi Hae-Chan*
> *Institute for Cell- and Neurobiology*
> *Charité Berlin*

And now she was gliding in this large grey limousine closer and closer to her destination. Why, for goodness sake, had she accepted this invitation? She couldn't quite explain it to herself. She remembered sitting in her armchair for hours in a daze, until it had become dark outside, and hadn't rationally weighed up the pros and cons of this venture at all.

A thunderstorm of images had run through her head, flashing all the possibilities of being, from new infatuation to endless infirmity, alternately bringing sweat to her forehead and cold shivers down her spine. Finally, she had resorted to red wine to take the sharpest edges and spikes out of her thoughts, which of course had gone grandly wrong in the end. She hadn't come to any decision until the driver's call, which had only been yesterday morning.

She was healthy, she felt well, she was mentally in top shape. She had every desire in the world to go on living, not only to proceed with her scientific work, but also, for example, to see her grandchildren grow up. She wanted to travel, maybe even to Seoul one day, to actually give her lectures there. Or take a trip into space on one of those new tourist spaceships.

Every day exciting things happened that were either good or bad, fruitful or devastating, but in any case interesting. For example, the recent victory of medicine over two scourges of mankind, cancer and multiple sclerosis. Or holographic television, plastic products produced on one's own PC printer, traces of life on Mars... not to mention the only just avoided meltdown at the San Onofre Nuclear Power Plant in California, which might have cost thousands of lives, and finally prompted the USA to rethink their policy of environmental protection.

There were so many new things that already existed, and so much more to come. Yes, she still wanted to experience a lot, wanted to know what would happen next, didn't want to just walk out in the middle of the film without knowing the end. Didn't a famous poet – wasn't it Elias Canetti? – say that death was nothing less than a scandal?

She wasn't sure, though, how she would cope if everyone around her grew older, and she didn't. If she had to watch Klara, her best friend, pass away, possibly after a serious illness like Thomas. Or, even worse, if her own daughters overtook her in the ageing process and were buried while she herself stood at their graves in the best of health. Is there anything worse than burying your own children?

Of course, perhaps she could arrange that her daughters would be the next to benefit from the therapy... and her sons-in-law... and her granddaughters with their relatives... Would she manage to avoid all the questions that were sure to arise – or to answer them with stock phrases?

She hardly noticed how the world around the car was gliding by more and more slowly, and only when it came to a halt with a gentle jolt did she wake up from her reverie and struggle back to the reality of the 11 motorway.

'A traffic jam?' she remarked anxiously.

'Don't worry, it won't be long,' the driver said. 'I can already see the construction site.'

'What are they building again?'

'They are laying induction lines. Have you heard of *Smacar*?'

'Isn't it called *Smart Car*?'

'Actually, it's called Smart Caravanning. It's about a power cable embedded in the roadway that takes over the control of the motor vehicles. They then automatically follow the cable without the driver having to intervene. He can sit back and take a nap or even stay at home.'

' Hmm… but hasn't that already been around for quite some time?' she asked in surprise.

'Yes, self-driving cars have actually been around for a longer time,' the driver confirmed. 'But remember how unpredictable they were. There were always crashes, and afterwards people argued about who was to blame… the owner, the manufacturer, the builder of the road… Anyway, then they came up with the idea of the cable. By the way, this car is already prepared for it. It has all kinds of sensors and automatic controls. But so far we are lacking the corresponding roads.'

'And that would be safer?'

'Yes and no. Besides the cable, there is a second system, a chain of transponders on the crash barriers, just to be on the safe side. Things never go as they should in the beginning. What would happen, for example, in a power cut?'

'Hmm… I see,' Irmgard murmured thoughtfully.

'If I had to pick you up in two years' time, I would possibly just send the empty car. But then you would have to take a taxi to the motorway. And vice versa in Berlin.'

'How convenient,' she wrily replied.

They reached the Berlin Ring, and Irmgard felt the scheduled meeting with Professor Yi was becoming more and more tangible reality. Her hopeful optimism began to fade and give way to a feeling of distress. It is not at all certain that everything will run smoothly, she thought. Nothing works right from the start. Should she perhaps see herself more as a victim than a pioneer? As a guinea pig?

It wouldn't even be necessary for the therapy to fail. Even if it worked wonderfully, there'd be numerous problems that no one was thinking about now. What would happen, for example, if she became ill? Or, more simply, if she had a serious accident that confined her to a wheelchair? Would she then be in it for fifty years or more? Where would that leave all her dreams for the future?

Last but not least: Who would actually pay for such a long-term care? Wouldn't the insurance companies refuse? Wouldn't they already do so in her case right now? After all, they had enough to do with the normal ageing of society. She imagined herself being cared for by a nice robot nurse who fetched her for dinner every evening with the words 'Have we done our research today?'. She found herself once again in the middle of a huge avalanche of heavy, black thoughts.

With thin lips, she observed how the buildings of the city became taller and denser. In Pankow, the motorway changed into a six-lane city street, and soon they turned right into Tor Straße, which led to Oranienburger Tor.

'We're almost there,' the driver remarked.

She pulled her handbag towards her, clutching it tightly.

'Can I ask you something?'

'Of course, go ahead.'

'What do you think about *eternal life*?'

The driver looked back, wondering. This was a question he rarely heard from his passengers. He concentrated on the traffic for a while before answering.

'When, now, or hereafter?'

'Now.'

'Hmm... does it have to be forever? But a few years wouldn't be bad, I guess.'

'Are you sure?'

The driver shrugged his shoulders. 'Well, let me say it this way: *Who really wants to die?*'

II

Gamma Flash

1.

Absolute blackness. Tiny points of light animate the nothingness, as if someone had drilled countless holes in a dark wall behind which a cold light was burning. There is no clear system apparent to the eye. In front of us a broad shimmering zone – the galaxy. As if made up of myriads of snow crystals, it shines rather reddish in some sectors and bluish in others. The lights are rigid; they do not sparkle at all. Along with the absolute silence, they intensify the feeling of all-encompassing indifference.

The panorama, however, harbours a small irregularity: stars are obscured by blackness for a moment, while yellowish lights tumble around each other on the same spot. A closer look reveals the spaceship, which, like a long tube, rotates around its own transverse axis. It is difficult to tell if it is moving forward. In fact, however, it hurries along at centilight-speed following a precisely calculated course that will lead it to new worlds in the near future.

The dimensions of the object are enormous. It consists of a framework more than three thousand metres long with various modules attached. In the middle of the tube, close to the rotation axis, are the fuel tanks. They take up about half the volume of the construction. The illuminated containers at the two ends contain the crew quarters. The force of the rotation creates an apparent gravity that allows people to move quite normally in their cabins. The crew consists of 675 humans of both sexes.

The spaceship flies completely autonomously. It was launched from orbit around Earth about 210 years ago, according to spacecraft time, and has since travelled a distance of four light years from Earth's position. Communication with the home planet is practically impossible.

2

The spaceship is called *Golden Promise*. It is owned by EURA, the Eurasian Union, which also operates other space travel projects – mostly within the solar system. The name of the ship is emblazoned in large Chinese and Latin characters on the fuel tanks. It alludes to the craft's mission: the conquest of new worlds. Its current aim is to advance to the star system *Alpha Centauri* and, if possible, to take possession of and colonise the newly discovered planet *Alpha Centauri Bd* for the Union.

The ship's travellers see themselves as a community, as their various duties and activities, in a way, resemble those of life in a small village. They consist entirely of durants, i.e., humans whose lifespan is continuously prolonged and thus can reach a thousand years or more. This procedure ensures the ship is spared from major upheavals, and constantly gains in knowledge and experience. Thus, it can be considered the embodiment of material and spiritual balance, an inert, rational organism with endlessly recurring cycles. There are neither children nor old people. The *durare technique* was applied to all community members at the age of thirty to forty. They remain at this age until their unforeseeable deaths.

Of course, the durare technique cannot prevent injuries or fatal accidents. If the worst comes to the worst and an astronaut is lost, a stock of deep-frozen embryos stands by as a substitute, and a large number of transplantable organs are available for less serious cases.

Artificially prolonged life is unquestionably the key to the project's realisation. All attempts in the past to enhance the power of spaceships, and thus enable shorter travel times that cover only a fraction of the human lifespan, ultimately failed because of the immense fuel consumption and the corresponding costs of the new propulsion systems. In contrast, extending the lives of the occupants is a neglectable cost factor.

Communication within the ship is largely done via small radio sensors called COMs. They look like skin-coloured buttons and are worn on the temples. With their assistance, people can make contact with each other – telepathically, so to speak; the control of the devices is purely mental. Instructions from the control centre are also transmitted in this way. In addition, a loudspeaker system and common computer technology are available for emergencies.

Such an emergency has just occurred.

3.

Wailing of sirens, people running around in confusion, in the dormitories they straighten up in their bunks and search for their COMs. It is hard to understand anything because all mental-electronic communication is widely drowned out by the constant noise. Fortunately, more detailed information soon appears on the screens: A plasma confector has failed, so the protection against cosmic radiation is no longer sufficient. This is especially true in Sector II for floors 46 to 81, outer cabins 8 to 18, which are only accessible with special permission. Further instructions would be announced shortly.

The people on the Golden Promise are panic-stricken and frightened. There has never been such an incident before. The ship's technology has been constantly maintained – what else could one do on a journey of nearly three hundred years? – and accordingly, only minor mishaps have occurred so far, mostly due to errors by the crew. The present event, however, seems to have a different dimension.

Dark forebodings of irreparable damage are doing the rounds. There is talk of an aberration from the determined course and the ship finally being lost in the vastness of interstellar space. Some remain silent, others shout at each other, and some faint and are taken to the infirmary by nursing robots. The Dao, the balance of cosmic forces in flux, the guiding principle of thought since the beginning of the journey and, as it were, the official religion of the ship, seems to have given way to wild confusion.

After a while, an invitation appears on the screens to re-attach the COMs and participate in a collective meditation. The people reluctantly obey and look for chairs, but there are not enough, so many take a seat on the floor. In their heads, they hear a voice intoning the sacred mantra Namo Sanghayah, and in monotonous tones they join in the chant.

Thus, the staff gradually calm down, if only to some degree. Speculation about a test alarm arises. Then a new announcement is made: People are asked to gather in Assembly Room I in Module 1 to receive new information. Calmly and serenely, they enter the four lifts, two of which are encapsulated for space conditions and serve as express shuttles to connect the ends of the ship.

In Assembly Room I there are chairs for all 675 members of the community. (The additional twenty seats are the subject of bizarre jokes, most of which revolve around irregular love affairs with aliens.) People greet each other likewise with trepidation or warmth; many have not seen each other for weeks. In fact, the alienation of the staff between the two ends of the spaceship is a problem the management tries to bridge with regular events to strengthen the sense of solidarity. For the moment this does not matter, however. Each one takes a seat. The large screen activates and shows the intro graphic, the constellation of Centaurus, with the double star Alpha Centauri, the destination of the journey.

The commander of the ship appears on the screen, a Chinese man. He has a friendly face and appears only slightly older than the other space travellers. His casual clothes indicate that this is not a serious occasion. He speaks in a calm voice, first reporting awkwardly on the progress the expedition has made so far, then holding out the prospect of reaching the target planet without any problems in exactly thirty-eight years. Finally, he gets down to business.

'… and one more thing, comrades, bold conquerors of earth and sky! As you all know, cosmic radiation is one of the main problems of our mission. It limits our speed of travel, it limits the duration of our stays outside the ship, it has an inevitably lethal effect on those who do not protect themselves. It is present everywhere in the cosmos, except in those places that are shielded in a special way. This is true, for example, for the Earth; here the magnetic field fulfils this function.

And you trust that our ship is also protected in a similar way! Rightly so, I assure you! The two staff modules of the ship, including the farms and some other units, i.e., the life support modules, or LSMs, are both cocooned in a powerful layer of plasma, which has the effect that the hard radiation is deflected around the containers and cannot reach the interior. You and I, we are completely safe in here. And now I come to our little complication, which is why we have called this meeting.

The plasma is highly volatile and must be held to the ship with special structures. That's what the 100-metre masts are for – the so-called *confectors* that our life support units are equipped with. Yes, if someone is outside with a shuttle, they can see them. The two ends of our ship look as spiky as chestnuts, or maybe sea urchins. At the tips of the masts are large aluminium spheres that generate permanent electromagnetic fields. They enclose the plasma cocoons from the outside and hold them firmly in their intended place. This is the normal working condition, and as we all know, it has operated smoothly for more than 200 years.

And now, as I have already indicated, one of these confectors has failed. Therefore, some plasma can escape at this point. So the protection in this sector is limited, which is why some crew quarters were recently evacuated.'

At this point, he pauses to check the effect of his words. He sees his audience as clearly on his monitor as they see him. Perhaps it is the passivity that has set in over centuries, perhaps it is the effectiveness of the meditation programme he has just conducted, or the general tension that keeps anyone from stirring in their seats. Everyone stares at the screen, waiting for further explanations.

The commander clears his throat and continues: 'There is still no complete clarity about the nature and cause of the damage. We have already sent up robots and received an initial overview. Apparently, the sphere was hit by a meteoroid and badly damaged. The on-board seismographs have indicated this impact. The video transmission shows a wide crack about one and a half metres long. It also appears slightly out of position. The mast appears not to be affected. Oh yes – and there has been a short circuit. The main fuse has shut down the confector.

I would like to stress that the damage is limited and there is no cause for concern. We are holding our course, the rotation of the Promise has been readjusted. As things are standing, the sphere will be functional again within the next few weeks. So I can reassure you: Everything is in the green.'

So only a locally limited damage! He can clearly see the relief on their faces. Satisfied with himself, he tackles the last part of the speech, which addresses his real concern. For this, he once again goes into details, lapses into a matter-of-fact tone, and comes to talk about the star that is closest to our sun: Proxima Centauri, the nearest in the constellation of Centaur.

'Proxi, the little sister of the two Alphas, is a so-called *red dwarf*, and as dwarfs often do, she tries everything to appear big and powerful. So every few months she blazes around with huge flares, shining twice as bright as normal and spewing out radiation of all kinds, including hard X-rays. So there are good reasons to be wary of this little sister! Now, Proxima Centauri is barely bigger than our planet Jupiter, so even the wildest eruption would be limited. That means there is no reason to panic! Nevertheless, it is appropriate to strive for the highest safety level on our ship. It follows that we must lose no time and quickly repair the current damage to the plasma shell.'

The people in the hall listen devoutly. The commander, watching them on his monitor, is certain that even the last part of his speech does not miss the intended effect. While his eyes wander from one person to the next, he is particularly interested in the flight engineers, especially those of the male sex. After a while, he notices that people are stirring again, thinking the speech is over.

'I must ask you to stay a little longer,' the commander continues. 'Just a short moment more. So it's about the repairs – unfortunately, we had to accept that they cannot be done entirely by robots. Robots can't get through the crack that the meteoroid has torn. But we have to get in there to secure the electrical connections before we replace the entire sphere. So we need manpower, a person who has already done field operations several times.'

The flight engineer in question perks up. The task seems appealing to him. He knows it's not easy; one needs a fair amount of experience to avoid being hurled into space by the rotation of the ship, or even damaging the spacesuit on the jagged edges of the rift. On the other hand, the work stages are clearly defined. He would fly to the sphere in a small shuttle, dock the vehicle there, and carry out the repairs. Done! The cosmic radiation would not matter for this brief moment.

He looks around. His comrades from flight engineering seem moved by similar thoughts. He hears the commander continue: 'I have decided not to simply order the task, but to assign it to a volunteer. I want him or her to perform the work with all their heart and senses – with full commitment for the sake of the whole! I don't need to mention that this performance will be rewarded…' Here he pauses to give emphasis to his words and lets his gaze wander over the audience. '… My God, now I did mention it after all… '

General laughter. People rise, stretch their legs, and talk to their friends. Our astronaut keeps to himself, he's always been a bit of an introvert. Then he takes the direct route to the command centre.

4.

While the shuttle with the astronaut is still standing quietly on the launch pad, the entire universe seems to rotate evenly around the spaceship. The glittering strip of the Milky Way follows this movement, as does the constellation of Centaurus. One of its light points has steadily grown in brightness during the long journey of the Golden Promise, and now already outshines all the other stars. It is not Proxima Centauri, the red dwarf, the nearest one, that the commander was talking about. Its glowing light is completely overpowered by the bright rays of its two sisters, Alpha Centauri A and B.

The shuttle's engine is running. The astronaut is hardly aware of what is happening around him. He tensely concentrates on the display units and waits for the launch clearance to come via his COM. His position is almost in the middle of the ship, where the centrifugal forces are lowest. When the clearance is finally given, he undocks his shuttle. As he slowly picks up speed and slips away into endless space, he is again seized by that feeling of bliss that was familiar to him from previous field missions… the sensation of complete weightlessness, of absolute detachment from the mother ship, of irrevocable fusion with the forces of space…

He is now no longer part of the spinning movement of the ship, and therefore must be careful not to be smashed by its rotating ends. In an elegant arc, he gains some distance and turns the shuttle around, so that he has the whole structure of the spaceship in view. A black silhouette against the blackest blackness, like that one littered with numerous position lights. He sees the life support modules with their spiky outgrowths, identifies the one labelled LSM 1, and begins to follow its circular path with the headlights on. Now he feels the centrifugal force again and turns his vehicle so that the mother ship seems to hover above his head. He recognises the damaged confector from the conspicuous slant of its sphere and programmes his shuttle for automatic approach. Soon he spots the gap that the meteoroid has torn, targets a point below it and commands the vehicle via COM to dock there firmly. While this is happening, he reports back to headquarters.

The work turns out to be more extensive than he had imagined from the commander's speech because now he has to follow the service regulations exactly. First step: attach the safety line to the spacesuit and the shuttle. Second step: check the functionality of the spacesuit. Third step: fold up the shuttle's canopy. Fourth step: activate the dumbbells with the magnetic pads. Fifth step: strap on the tool bag. Sixth step: Carefully climb through the gap into the interior of the sphere. Use the magnetic suckers and be careful not to damage the spacesuit or the safety line.

It is completely dark inside the sphere. He switches on the handheld spotlight; its light is reflected criss-cross by the shiny aluminium walls. He looks at the place above his head where the sphere is connected to the holding mast. There is a conglomeration of cables, plug connections, sensors and measuring devices, computers and unused equipment sockets. By sucking to the metal wall with the help of the dumbbells, he crawls hand over hand to this functional group to take a closer look at it. He cannot see any irregularity in the electrics, however. With difficulty, he moves to the other side. Again, no visible damage, and certainly not the scorch marks of a short circuit! Mentally, he asks the control centre for advice and gets the tip to check the voltage of all power conductors. In fact, the result is negative for all but one. It is the one that is directly connected to the sphere shell and normally has the function of building up the charge. In his head, he hears excited discussions going on in the control centre. From the buzz of voices, he finally understands that the measured voltage is not too high but too low. Since the sphere is influenced by the electromagnetic fields of the neighbouring confectors, it must have a clear charge. But this is only present in traces, which indicates the current is leaking out somewhere other than inside the confector.

The astronaut senses a feeling of frustration. He stows away the gauges and drops one metre 'down" onto the lower spherical wall, which would not be a problem on Earth but is strictly forbidden in this situation. He decides to examine the outer shell of the confector once more – perhaps the robots have missed something.

Back in his shuttle, he circles around the end of the confector, his headlights focused on the sphere. His eyes slowly wander to the supporting mast, and there he sees it: The ceramic insulation ring between the sphere and the mast tube has been damaged by the collision, a piece has broken out. The ball may have a short circuit at this point, he thinks. Carefully, he steers his vehicle closer to the construction and finally docks. The damage is exactly at the angle between the mast and the sphere, difficult to see from the shuttle's point of view. So he opens the canopy once more, and while doing so, he notices that he has forgotten the adhesive dumbbells inside the sphere. He utters an angry curse, which is also noticed in the control centre, and causes some hilarity there. If everything else fails, he reassures himself, he still has the safety line. He leaves his vehicle and now squats on the sphere in the bright shine of the headlights, the mast in front of him, the docked shuttle behind him. Held down by the centrifugal force of the spacecraft, he crawls a few steps forward and now realises the full extent of the damage. The slanted sphere has crushed the insulation ring and then touched the end of the support mast. The short-circuit has melted away a fist-sized piece of the sphere, splashing drops of metal in all directions. Perfectly clear why the main fuse had immediately shut down the confector. In the control centre, they see what the astronaut sees and joyfully confirm to him that his mission is now complete.

The astronaut feels relieved. He carefully turns around, sits down in front of the mast, and allows himself a break. He notices the hissing of his breath in his helmet again, and feels his pulse slowing down with each beat. As the tension in his body fades, he shuts his eyes from the shuttle's glaring headlights and gradually comes to rest. Mentally, he switches off his COM. After a while, pleasant memories come back to him, images from his time on Earth, his mother, not yet in a wheelchair at the time, the family home on the outskirts of the city. His sister, the bitch he had to rescue from the tree. His admired father, rarely at home. Something about these memories makes him ponder, he opens his eyes and stares ahead. Blinded by the shuttle's headlights, he sees – or rather suspects – the firmament wandering endlessly in the same direction. The position lights of the ship above him – motionless. The sagging safety line is gently swinging back and forth, reliably connecting him to his spacecraft.

A faint glow gently brushes past his shuttle, and it seems to him as if the spacecraft has dimly flickered in this light. He turns his eyes upwards, but does not realise that some position lights have gone out. At the same time, he unconsciously notices how the shuttle's headlights go down and then come on again. As he becomes finally aware that something must be wrong with the machine, a shiver runs through his body, and his pulse begins to race. He is horrified to see that his vehicle has detached itself from the spherical casing and is swaying lightly in front of him with the canopy open. He has no explanation, he only knows that this is a monstrous event. Mortal fear grows within him. His body cramps. He sits rigid, incapable of any thought. Meanwhile, the distance between the sphere and the tumbling vehicle gets bigger and bigger. The safety line, slack just a few moments ago, begins to straighten out. His subconscious, rather than he himself, sees only two options left: to make a daring jump and save himself in the shuttle with the help of the safety line, or to cut the line and stay on the confector. According to the regulations, the former would probably be advisable. However, the behaviour of the shuttle does not seem very encouraging, it seems downright hostile.

Now the rope tightens. It tugs at his outfit and threatens to tear him from the confector by force. So he pulls the panic hook and releases the line.

Still sitting, he clings to the welded seams of the sphere; he manages to slide all the way back to the mast and, reaching back with his arms, finds a makeshift hold. His thoughts are dancing wildly, straining to find a way to turn the situation around, perhaps reach the shuttle that is veering furiously in front of him, plunging him alternately into glaring light and dim darkness – but something stops him from making the ultimate leap. He watches as the vehicle suddenly veers off and drifts out into empty space in tumbling swings, as if guided by a ghost's hand, finding its way between the confectors.

He realises that this practically seals his death. He could just as easily get up, jump off his sphere and follow the shuttle into the infinite blackness. The alternative would be: stay put and watch the rotating universe, until the reserves of his spacesuit are exhausted and he suffocates or freezes to death. This would be the case in two hours at the latest. Suddenly, the fear becomes so great that he no longer senses it and feels weirdly free. The question of universal meaning abruptly sweeps through his thoughts, perhaps for the first time in his life. What was the point, he thinks, of all this effort? What was the point of his deprived training, what was the point of the constant life-prolonging measures, of maintaining a neurologically defined balance, of following the *Jin and Jang*, if the whole project of life – no, simply of his own life – is to be terminated through such a trivial event?

He feels feverish.

He wonders if anyone in the mothership has even noticed his accident. He remembers his COM and listens inwardly to make contact with the control centre. Nothing there to be heard or seen, his mind remains blank. He doesn't even know if his COM is still in the right place. Nevertheless, he tries: 'Communication – on!' His command has no effect. Once more: 'Communication – on!' Again: nothing. 'Emergency! Emergency! Communication – on! On! On! Oooonnn!!!'

Nothing at all.

He lifts his gaze to the mothership. All lights have gone out.

5.

Sometime in the first hundred years of the journey, our astronaut had a discussion with his friend Jeanny. It was about the extinction of the dinosaurs.

'The dinosaurs died out because of an asteroid impact,' he said. 'That's the popular theory. The dust kicked up by the blast darkened the sunlight, the plants withered, and most living creatures were left to starve miserably. ...I don't believe all that.'

'But why not?' said Jeanny. 'It's very plausible, isn't it?'

'Sure, it's plausible. I'm not saying it couldn't have been that way. But this hypothesis is far too much based on what the evidence can prove, what the tools of the archaeologists' and geologists' trade can bring to light by means of bones and deposits. But there are also other possibilities. Explanations that can't be proved or tested in material reality.'

'And what would that be, smart alec?'

'Plagues, for example. Diseases that only dinosaurs died of, because they were the only ones who couldn't produce antibodies. Can you imagine an archaeologist holding up the skeleton of a virus to the camera and saying: 'That's the one?'' Hardly. Or organic weaknesses, weaknesses in the immune system. Allergies. Sensitivity to specific environmental toxins.'

'All pretty speculative, don't you think?'

'But the other is just too good to be true. Listen, dinosaurs populated all sorts of biotopes – and densely populated them! – from the air to the land to the open sea, and in all sizes. Some species even burrowed in the ground like moles! And all of them have become extinct! Unlike many species that had only a narrowly defined habitat and limited survival abilities – the crocodiles and many other reptiles, for example.'

'I see, so the asteroid didn't do it. And what do you think it was?'

'I think it was a *gamma flash*!'

6.

Of course, everyone on board knows what gamma flashes are. But although minor impacts were recorded almost daily on the spaceship, they were rarely the subject of technical discussion. They are not talked about – perhaps because they are somehow unspecific due to their light nature, but perhaps also because their occurrence is so sudden and inescapable. They are products of cosmic catastrophes and race through space at the speed of light, sometimes devastating, sometimes barely measurable, no warning is possible. Some protection from the deadly radiation is provided – similar to the Earth's magnetic field – by the plasma shields, which, held in place by the confectors, wrap themselves around the life-support modules of the spaceship.

7.

Brightly whitewashed walls, dim warm light. The room is far too big for the white bed that stands in it. If it weren't for the apparatus at its head, the smell of medication would indicate that this is a hospital room.

By the standards of a spaceship, it is downright cosy: It has a large round carpet that defies all hygiene regulations, pictures on the wall, and a large ceiling lamp that would have done honour to any earthly living room. The outstanding feature, however, is one wall, which in fact is a huge screen that offers the bedridden person a view of a magnificent – albeit motionless – panorama: a Swiss mountain landscape. To the left, chamois rush over the rocks; in the air, a golden eagle flies. In the distance, between meadows and forests, you can see a road and a village.

The room is silent, except for the eternal murmur of the supply systems and the ticking sounds of the medical apparatus.

The person in the bed is almost completely wrapped in bandages. Only his eyes, nose and mouth are exposed. He seems badly injured. Judging by the bandages, he has suffered severe burns. A woman is sitting next to the bed, her hand gently resting on the patient's arm. He does not notice all this; pain-relieving medication is constantly fed to him through an infusion tube.

Apart from the two people, there is another person in the room: a nursing robot, or more precisely, an android. He crouches inconspicuously on a stool in a corner, in standby mode.

The sick person turns his eyes to the visitor by his bed and says softly, 'Thank you.'

She shakes her head. 'You don't have to keep on thanking me. I really enjoyed doing that.'

'You did more than you had to. A lot more.'

'Possibly. But what was I supposed to do? I couldn't leave you sitting out there, could I?'

'I told you to look after the farms. They were in the dark and cooling down more and more. The whole crop of LSM 16 was in danger.'

'That's true, but after half an hour, the worst was over.'

'And you were the only one of the whole team who thought there was still someone else roaming around in the cosmos, and you came looking for me.'

She involuntarily grips her temple. She has put down her COM so that she can talk to her friend undisturbed. 'I only became restless when I couldn't get in touch with you. The COM wasn't working.'

'All the COMs went down, I heard.'

'Yes, but they worked again after a short while. Only yours didn't.'

The sick astronaut sighs. 'Yeah, wonder why? I guess I got hit a little harder outside than you did in here. The protective shield for the inhabited modules was essentially intact.'

'Exactly. Except for where you were.'

The memory of that makes him visibly uncomfortable. He rolls his eyes and tries to straighten up. 'Believe me, it was horrible, all alone on that sphere. I had already left everything behind. And then, suddenly… your shuttle appears, way in the back…'

'Shh, don't get excited! Lie back again.'

He smiles at her and lets himself sink back onto the cushions.

Then he asks, 'Do we know exactly yet what really happened?'

'Well. What do you think it was? You talked to me about it once. It was a *gamma flash*!'

'Oh no!'

She bites her lips. She had thought he had been clear about that. But obviously he hadn't. Then maybe he also doesn't know how severe his injuries really are. They are so severe that it is pointless to replace the damaged organs. The surgical skills of the medical android team can perform miracles, but in this case they are powerless. Everything would have to be replaced, including the brain. But that would only be a cynical euphemism for a matter that was thought to have been overcome long ago.

Death.

8.

'It can't be!'

The astronaut sits up in bed and stares straight ahead, as if he sees an explanation there. 'But I didn't feel anything! You'd feel something like that! Besides, there were no omens! Are you sure it wasn't a flare? A flare from Proxima Centauri?'

'Sorry, sorry… of course it could have been anything…'

'I was out for such a short time, ten minutes at most… it's just too unlikely this lightning struck at that exact moment… it's completely impossible!'

'Maybe you're right. But something must have done it.'

'And who says it was a lightning? Who spreads stupid rumours like that?'

'Headquarters.'

'And where do they get their wisdom? Did the equipment record anything like that?'

'There… you ask me too much. I don't know.'

He smiles at her. 'Well, we can find out. Give me my COM. Or even better, Andro!'

The care android in the corner comes to life. His coloured diodes sparkle, he stands up measuredly and rolls up to the bed. His shiny white figure is roughly the shape of a human being, or rather, a caricature of one.

'Andro! Here's what I want to know,' says the astronaut. 'What irregular event has occurred in the last two days?'

The android pauses for a moment, as he always does when asked a question. He scours all the networks and files as fast as he can to find the best answer. He is also linked to the COM network but does not have access to some classified information. Finally, the clicking and whirring in his chest subside, and he launches into an endless litany, featuring an accurate listing of all the defects and failures within all the modules of the Golden Promise.

'Andro!' The astronaut interrupts him. 'I mean: an event that affected the ship from the outside!'

'… Eighteen-eleven spacecraft time: extreme increase in short-wave radiation for about six minutes. Failure of all electrical systems, partial failure of backup systems, failure of the COM network…'

'Give us more information on the increase in radiation!'

'Eighteen-eleven-34 spacecraft time: sudden increase in radiation energy in the range of 0.05 to 8.2 picometers. Energetic peak at about 1.2 megaelectronvolts. Decay at about eighteen-sixteen-fourteen spacecraft time. Afterglow with longer wavelength still persisting.'

'And no error possible?' asks the astronaut. 'I mean, the devices were down, weren't they? They could have recorded anything.'

'The devices were still intact at the time of impact. They only failed shortly afterwards when the whole system was overloaded.'

Paralysing silence. Slowly, the sick man lets himself sink back onto the pillows. Jeanny sends the android back to his corner.

'I shouldn't have been sent out!' he complains. 'They should have tried once more with a robot! If only because of the flares from Proxima Centauri!'

'So you're saying it's the headquarters' fault,' Jeanny says.

'Of course! They had all the information. They might have known that such an event was imminent. As I said, just because of the flares... and you – they let you out too. You've probably got some too.'

'But I stayed in my cabin, underneath the open cover. I just threw the safety line over to you. You hooked on and then pulled yourself aboard.'

His attempt to find a fellow sufferer in her failed. 'So lucky,' he whispers.

Another long silence as she holds his hand. He closes his eyes and turns his head away. A tear rolls down his nose. 'I'll call Andro again,' he says. 'I want to know how serious the injuries are and what happens now.'

'I can tell you that too. It is what it is.'

'So *exitus*!'

'Holger! We've examined you from top to bottom. You got over ten sieverts. You know what that means.'

'Of course I know. You have made it crystal clear by now!'

'Sorry, I thought...'

'You thought I was supposed to come to terms with reality.' She nodded.

'So now we wait for a miracle.'

36

'Do you believe in eternal life?'

'There is always a way,' she replied.

'I don't mean your Dao wisdom. I am not interested in cryptic phrases or flowing energies here. But to stay with your image of the path: Aren't some paths dead ends? Or do you think the house at the end of the alley is not locked, and one can pass through and then get onto a new street?'

She feels uncomfortable with his question, and the image of the dead-end-alley being permeable confuses her completely.

'I understand,' he concedes, 'you still have many, perhaps hundreds of years ahead of you. So the question of the hereafter is not exactly burning on your mind.'

'I believe in the Dao, the constant conflict of Jin and Jang, which brings about an eternal balance after all.' She recites it like a student in an exam.

'Sure, sure, our spaceship religion. This idea suits people who practically live forever – live in this world, I mean. Just stay cool! Always keep your inner balance, don't jeopardise the continuous life for which you have spent so much effort! But what will you do if it doesn't work out? If you end up at the just mentioned dead end? Will you sit down and meditate?'

She smiles meaningfully. 'That probably wouldn't be the worst idea. Quietly wait and see what comes. Just let it happen. Anything is possible. Even the afterlife.'

'That would be death with dignity, at least,' he says, lapsing into brooding silence.

'Well, that's not enough for me, a death in dignity,' he says after a while.

'And in peace, don't forget that.'

'Listen: When a chicken is killed so that we can have meat, no one cares about what its soul does afterwards. No one is afraid of meeting the spirit of the chicken now, or even after death, and possibly being called to account. If the chicken is dead, then in our eyes it is over and done with, basta! Just like a mosquito that we have killed. Why not the same with humans?'

'The Dao is the same for all living things.'

'That's what the spaceship religion says. But most people don't see it that way. I wonder why we claim such a special treatment for us humans? Is it fear? Are we so afraid of dying that we agree with any self-deception? Is it that? Does desire for life just force the image of endless living on us?'

'Wouldn't it be a beautiful image: We land on Alpha Centauri Bd, and you are there in spirit. We take possession of the planet, and you are there. You can even help us build our colony from beyond the grave.'

'That's exactly what I mean: wishful thinking!'

'So, to get back to your question from earlier: I believe in life continuing after death.'

'Er… why so suddenly?'

'Well… it just seems absurd to me that something as complex as a human being, next to which even the most expensive android seems like a puppet – that such a wonderful work of art should just pass away. It wasn't created for that purpose.'

'Created?'

'Well… You know the jokes. Someone shakes the universe vigorously, and by chance the atomic particles join together to form a spaceship. That's impossible. At least that's what I believe. And it would be the same with humans, only much less likely.'

'Hmm…'

'Would you like something to drink?' the sonorous voice of the nursing robot interjects. He must have reacted to the word most expensive android and moved unnoticed to the bedside. 'Coke, juice, water?'

'Do you want anything?' asks Jeanny. 'I think you should drink a lot!'

'All right. A beer, if possible.'

'Beer only on cosmic holidays.'

'So practically never. All right. Water then.'

Jeanny wants nothing, and the android pulls away.

'He can live forever if he's properly maintained,' says the astronaut. 'Practically, though, he only lives until the new model comes out.'

'What's wrong?' Andro stopped and turned his head one hundred and eighty degrees.

'No sparkling water, please,' the astronaut shouts.

10.

Jeanny has stood up and steps to the porthole. Among all the stars passing by the window, the double star Alpha Centauri stands out brightly. Her sister Proxima Centauri is still caught in her glow.

'Soon we'll be at our destination,' she says. 'It'll only be a few more years before we swing into orbit.'

'Honestly, it feels good to know that the Golden Promise is living up to its name.' He takes a deep breath. 'Even though I won't be there. Although… I'm feeling a little better at the moment.' Talking to his girlfriend is obviously doing him good. The flickering feeling that had gripped his whole body has subsided. At that moment, with a soft hiss, the automatic door opens, and the android comes in with a tea trolley, on which there is a bottle of mineral water and a glass.

'Here you go, non-carbonated water.' He pours the glass half full in consummate waiter style, while his diodes are sparkling mysteriously. 'Do you need anything else?'

The astronaut replies no, and the android disappears back into his corner with a wish for a speedy recovery.

'Is the glass half full or half empty now?' asks Jeanny, trying to change the subject. She sits by his bed again and smiles mischievously.

'I can tell you exactly: It's half full.'

'And why not half empty?'

'Because it depends on what you're aiming at. Full or empty. Andro poured me the glass half full, not half empty.'

'I see…'

'So if you pour me the glass completely full now and I drink half of it, then it's not completely empty yet, but half. Half empty.'

Half empty, the word lingers in the room. Suddenly, they both realise that the pun has gone awry and the fun has turned serious. That they were only circling the precarious situation of the patient. Not quite empty – but soon…

11.

The sick man stares at the ceiling. 'I have another question.'

'And what is that?'

'Do you believe in God?'

'In a higher being? Well, I certainly believe the idea of a God would not necessarily clash with our spaceship religion, as you call it.'

'I see. And what does that mean?'

'Well, well, I can imagine there are beings in space that are much more highly developed than we are. Why should our civilisation be the oldest in the cosmos?'

'So you think there are aliens somewhere who are smarter than us? All right, that's not what I'm talking about. I'm talking about a more powerful person, one who is beyond the laws of nature, who can even interfere with those laws. Who may also be able to influence our destiny. Do you believe in that?'

'Err… I can imagine it exists. However, this idea includes the fact that our minds are too primitive to recognise it.'

'That is correct.' Yet he still does not seem satisfied with this answer. 'But I mean something else. Let me put it this way: I mean the good old bearded man in paradise who strokes my head and says 'there, there'' when I am unwell, who cares for my earthly happiness and graciously takes me back into his arms when the time comes. Do you believe in him?'

'Shall I be honest?'

'If possible…'

'Well – probably not. This idea seems too artificial to me. That would just be pure wishful thinking…'

'You see! But it's precisely this figure that matters. Let the aliens or the omnipotent light beings whizz through space and do what they want. Let them strike at us with black matter and lightning, let them also dump masses of stars or our ship in black holes – from all this we can only assume they don't care about us. They don't care about our fate. So we can pray all we want.'

'That means…'

'That means only the old man comes into question. The *Good Lord*. Anything else would be nothing worth believing in.'

Jeanny thinks.

'Well, do you believe in him?' he insists.

'What do you want to hear?'

'That to believe in him would be to mock the human spirit. That it would be downright embarrassing to even think of such a homemade idol! That death cannot be dignified if you raise the white flag on your deathbed. That's what I want to hear!'

She almost cringes when she sees his angry gaze from the narrow opening that the head bandage leaves.

'Well, yes, but what does that leave us with?' she asks, concerned.

'I will find out in the time I have left. Perhaps just dignity after all?'

'Why do you make it so difficult for yourself? It comes as it comes. You should calm down. Shall we meditate together?'

He shakes his head. 'I'm glad you were here, Jeanny. Sorry for being so negative. Will you leave me alone now?'

Jeanny is far from pleased with how her visit went. She has not been able to comfort him, and even worse, she has allowed him to infect her with his scowling manner. She is almost glad he wants her to leave. The questions are too strange to her, too irrelevant, she does not feel comfortable in these spheres. She wonders how quickly she gets up. 'Well then, see you tomorrow.'

'Very well. Until tomorrow.'

'And get bet… good night to you.'

'You too.'

12.

When she has left, he calls the android over to him. 'Andro: I would like to hear some music. Maybe something classical.'

'Something classical. Just a moment…'

'Just pick something nice. You know what it's about.'

The apparatus sparkles and rolls away thoughtfully.

'Oh Andro!' the astronaut calls after him. 'And turn on the video!' After all his harsh words, he feels the need for something comforting, even if it were something completely useless, like the memory of his mother or a song he heard as a child. If dignity is no longer possible, he thinks, there is always comfort…

The picture on the wall comes to life. The chamois finally climb their rock, and the eagle cries through the air. Mountains and valley suddenly seem to become reality. Now *Handel's Largo*, which Andro has chosen, begins with a soft, undulating sound, and a beautiful baritone voice sings:

> *Ombra mai fu*
> *Di vegetabile*
> *Cara ed amabile*
> *Soave più…*

13.

Absolute blackness. Tiny points of light animate the nothingness, as if someone had drilled holes in a black wall. They are rigid; they do not sparkle, and thus intensify the feeling of all-encompassing indifference.

Barely visible in the darkness, a spaceship follows its straight course. It will soon enter braking mode. In about thirty-eight years, it will reach its destination.

So far, the project has registered no personnel losses – except for one. But a single casualty in 210 years – one of 675 durants – that can undoubtedly be considered a good result.

III

Bomb Deposit

1.

Käfer hated these ceremonies. To him, they were nothing more than disruptions to his daily routine. Sure, many would have given anything to see the rich of this world up close. Like Ella, his cousin, for example. For her, there was nothing more uplifting than basking in the glow of some royal celebrity. She used almost every free minute to watch *Aristocrats' Channel* on television. Expensive pay-TV, mind you! And this in the middle of the twenty-first century! Well, if you were of such little importance yourself… For his part, he had given up television at all. He found the programmes just too stupid, and for a biochemist there was hardly anything to watch. He might just as well stand in the station hall and watch the people's busy bustle. Or, like today, in the reception hall of the DURATEC company.

The hall was not very large, but still much more spacious than the company's other meeting rooms. It was sparsely furnished – a lectern in front of three semi-circular rows of seats for the notabilities, expensive damask curtains on the walls, and a large silk Peking carpet on the parquet floor. The whole arrangement crowned by four small candelabras. They were on even though the room was bright as day. All in all, not a place where scientists really feel at home. Most of Käfer's colleagues had already arrived and stood in groups near the walls.

Käfer walked up to them and grimaced. Another hour, at least, of working time wasted for nothing, paralysing the whole company! And all this just to kowtow to more or less respectable (more the latter, thought Käfer) filthy rich bigwigs. Like in the Middle Ages, he thought. Where have we got to! We're marching back along the timeline, at top speed. Magnis itineribus, a vague memory of his Latin class at school, came to his mind.

'Who is it today?' he asked the group.

'Mswati the Fifth,' said Klara Mundt, the head secretary. She was small, a little plump, but still well built by Käfer's standards. He liked her.

'Aha! Now it's clear.'

'King of Swaziland. Poor but sexy. The citizens, not him. He's really loaded. Supposed to be one of the richest princes in the world.'

'If it's money earned honestly…'

'No question! As long as he leaves it with us…'

'He will! And it will be a pretty little sum, for sure.'

The group at the door began to move. The employees of the ICN, the Institute for Cell and Neurobiology, streamed in. The ICN was part of the Charité, the big academic hospital of Berlin. The institute resided in the same building as DURATEC and had many connections with it. Apparently, the executives wanted to roll out for the African potentate a grand red carpet. All that was missing was a flag to wave for each one, thought Käfer.

An hour later, when the conversation was running out and most of them were already stepping from one foot to the other, the time had finally come. Those who had expected an African chief like from a musical show found themselves disappointed: a black-skinned man in a normal dark suit entered. He was rather small, a little roundish and of middle age. Only the three favourite women in his entourage, who towered over him by a head, gave a halfway exotic impression. Their outfits, however, were more Parisian haute couture than African lore. Like his predecessors, Mswati stuck to tribal traditions to an extent that would have done credit to Louis the Fourteenth, the French Sun King. Only in one respect did he make an exception: He did not want to join his ancestors and conduct the business of a ghost when his time was ripe. Whatever the cost, he wanted to prolong his earthly life up to one hundred and fifty, if medically possible. At full manhood, of course. And by then, he told himself, the philosopher's stone would be found that would give him eternal life. Käfer wondered whether Mswati would also grant this favour to his three favourite women. Probably they had tried to persuade him in this sense, without any illusions about their future life together with him.

This was more or less the intention of everyone who came from wherever to DURATEC in Berlin: managers of big companies, financial tycoons, association officials, politicians, footballers, film stars. The Forbes list of billionaires provided a good selection of potential candidates because treatment with DURA technology was expensive, very expensive. The company kept quiet about how expensive exactly, just as it strived to avoid any publicity at all. Not because their activities might seem dubious, but because they took the view, in accordance with the political elite, that the time was not yet ripe for mass application. And that was it. After all, no client had attracted attention yet because of their exorbitantly long lives. The run-up had been too short for that.

Today, the attendance of celebrities in the audience was rather sparse in view of the restrained ethical standards of the potentate. Only the CEO of DURATEC, Prof. Dr. Renemult, entered the room with him, together with Kretschmann, head of the foreign trade department of the Berlin Chamber of Commerce and Industry, then an unnamed official of the Ministry of Development and a likewise little-known businessman who probably had some trade relations to Swaziland. So the third row of chairs remained empty.

The reception ceremony got underway and proceeded precisely like the day before, when a CEO of a global IT company had arrived. And that again was almost exactly the same as in the previous week – in short, it was a well-functioning routine. Renemult held the welcoming speech, highlighting genetic medicine and thereby especially the achievements of ICN and DURATEC. Mswati the Fifth praised the good business relations between Swaziland and the newly refounded EU, while one of his favourite women buckled her stiletto heel and spilled the champagne that had been served in the meantime.

Käfer tried hard to stifle a yawn. He let his half-closed eyes wander to Dr. Mejul Sirlana, the head of the diagnostics department – also a functioning routine. Today she was wearing a burgundy costume. It went wonderfully with her shiny black hair, Käfer thought. Unfortunately, she was involved with Lasis, the head of the pharmacy, who was quite a scoundrel in Käfer's eyes. Sirlana would be the first to get her hands on Mswati, that is, one male member of her staff, because in the preliminary talks Mswati had strictly refused to be examined by a woman. This initial check-up would be about the physical condition of the client, in particular focussing on his tendency to malignant tumours. (*Client* instead of *patient*, since the visitors did not come because they were ill.)

Not only these possible side effects of the DURA technique, but also a completely different factor caused the staffs of DURATEC and ICN to be slightly less sleepy than usual. Mswati would be the first to be treated with the updated release of the DURA technology, version DT-3.4. It made it no longer necessary to treat the client first as an in-client for a few days and then as an out-client for a few more weeks. Except for the very first treatment, DT-3.4 was entirely self-medicated by the client. That simply meant adding another blue item to his daily colourful cocktail of pills.

2.

After King Mswati the Fifth of Swaziland and his mistresses had been escorted out of the reception hall to be taken back to their residence in the Grand Hotel Adlon, the staffs of the two companies slowly returned to their corridors and workrooms. Käfer adjusted his steps in a way that, as if by chance, he came to walk next to Sirlana. He gathered all his charm, a rather futile attempt, and addressed her from the side.

'Hello, Mejul. Do you have a minute?'

Sirlana seemed torn out of deep thought. She turned her dark dreamy eyes to him, and Käfer melted away.

'Hey, Bernd. What's up?'

'I've finished the text for the press release. I thought maybe you could give it a quick skim?'

'Hmm… I actually have to prepare for our king. You know, he's coming to see us in diagnostics first.'

'Oh… tomorrow already?'

'No, the day after tomorrow. Tomorrow he wants to visit the automobile show.'

'Come on, then. Then it can't be so urgent.'

They arranged to meet in the cafeteria next to the roof terrace. Käfer took a diversion via his office to fetch the note, while Sirlana walked directly to the lift.

*

The cafeteria was almost completely filled. The colleagues, like Käfer, felt the need to recover from the strains of complete inactivity during the reception, and had, after its closure, stormed the location en masse. Käfer let his eyes wander, but Sirlana was nowhere to be seen. Only when he reached onto the open roof terrace did he spot her sitting at a small table on the railing, squinting into the distance.

The closer urban view was not particularly spectacular by Berlin standards – the usual concrete blocks, some higher than their own building, all more or less futuristic, more or less equipped with alternative energy technology, more or less occupied by companies and institutes of the biotechnology and genetic engineering sector. DURATEC and ICN were located in the middle of the new Technology Park BIOBIG, affectionately called "Monsterfelde" by the Berliners. Its facilities spread across the site of the former Tegel Airport, which had been reduced to two short runways and a tiny terminal reserved exclusively for private jets. Mswati had also landed here.

Käfer saw that she had not yet picked up anything. 'What can I get you?' he asked, placing the draft press release on the table. 'A crimsato, perhaps?'

She nodded, Käfer disappeared and returned after a short while with a latte macchiato and coffee crimsato.

He sat down, trying to cope with the force of her radiance on him, while she gazed at the planes taking off and landing. They showed up in the gaps between the concrete blocks at frequent intervals.

'There may be our next customers coming already,' he remarked as calmly as he could while stirring the beautiful layering of his drink with the long spoon.

'Gönnerwein,' she said, 'Central Executive Officer of TAUCETICS.'

'Never heard.'

'TAUCETICS – space tourism. I doubt the company will ever fly to Tau Ceti, though. The star is twelve lightyears away, I think. But one is supposed to aim high, after all, to make small progress at least.'

'Like we did?'

She took a meaningful silent sip of her blood-red coffee.

'We have a fine job after all,' she said.

'No doubt,' said Käfer. 'Except for these sickening receptions. Soon I will be able to sleep standing upright.'

'So you have developed a thick skin that keeps you vertical. But don't worry, I'm no different.'

Käfer felt nervous (as he always did in her presence) and wondered whether her remark could be turned into a slight insinuation such as 'I'd like to put your thick skin to the test', or something similar. But then he decided to leave it at that.

'The clients would still come without all this fuss, I tell you,' she continued. 'Life extension is no fun. It's serious. They'd even kill for it without thinking twice.'

Käfer nodded thoughtfully. 'It's better the press keep it on a low flame. Once the masses realise what it's all about – my goodness, that would be hell on earth!'

While he spoke, Sirlana raised her cup to him a little higher than normal, affirming his words. 'But you just wrote a press release,' she said. 'In it, you describe exactly what it is about!'

'Well, the press department requested it that way. And I formulated it how I see it as a scientist and how it is factually correct. They'll make something out of it. I'd bet that when they issue the statement, there will be nothing left of the original meaning. Neither life extension nor genetic engineering. Everyone will think it's an advertisement for a new instant cat food.'

She laughed her brilliant laugh, and all his excitement gave way to a feeling of composure, an emotion he knew from his own lectures when he had found the first words. It was the 'it's-going-now-as-it-goes-feeling' with the prospect of a satisfying ending.

'So I think the explanation is good,' she said, picking up the sheet again. 'It's just that I find the wording with the three bases very confusing, at least for geneticists. Everyone knows that DNA is formed by four bases: A,G,T,C. But you mean the three main fields of the DURA technique: continuation of cell division, intensification of cell repair and prevention of cancer. I would rather call these *foundations* or *pillars*. Yes, the three pillars of the DURA technique!'

'And another pillar is coming soon, my new field of work: *rejuvenation*. But it's too soon to talk about it yet.'

A shadow loomed over them and asked, 'May I join you?' Neither had seen Lasis coming. He leaned over Sirlana and gave her a kiss, which was a little fiercer than Käfer, who spontaneously looked away, was wanting to stand.

Lasis was tall and slender, rather gaunt, and had pronounced eye brows that did not match his short, crooked nose at all. He would have made an excellent cast in a Dracula film, Käfer thought, with his long, anthracite-coloured coat. It was probably his dynamic, resolute air that attracted women. And this not very infrequently in the past, as Käfer recalled.

Sirlana knew nothing about his womanising; she had only been with the company for a few weeks. Maybe she didn't want to know either. It had always been a mystery to Käfer why beautiful, interesting women threw themselves into the arms of such rude fiends like Lasis. Sure, he himself was rather average-looking, medium height, slightly pug and somewhat introverted, nothing unusual for a scientist – good standard after all. Admittedly, his name was way more than plain. Käfer[1]. Just imagine they were married: Mejul Käfer! But even then: not at all attractive?

Lasis pulled up a chair with a crash and sat down. Turning to Sirlana, he said, 'I hear our friend from Africa doesn't want you to examine him? A gross mistake, I'd say!' This Dr. Mabuse face could actually smile, even quite charmingly, and Sirlana went for it.

Käfer was still labouring at the fact that Lasis hadn't given him a glance so far, and said a little too loudly: 'Nice to see you again, dear colleague!', which, however, only inspired him to a disinterested eyelid shrug.

'In any case,' Lasis said, 'I wouldn't mind if one of his favourite women... provided she had a doctorate and was a proven expert on... on...'

'Digital sex-genetics?' Käfer helped.

'Wow! Colleague! I didn't know what interesting special fields of genetics there are! And that you know all about them!'

'Maybe he's one of those famous still waters?' speculated Sirlana. 'But why should one of the favourite women examine you? You've already been through it all.'

That was true. Lasis, like all the DURATEC employees and most of the ICN, was already durated. To emphasise her words, she pointed to her left shoulder blade where the transponder was implanted. The STATRAY, which reported data about the individual's state of health to DURATEC via radio call.

At that moment, Lasis's mobile phone rang. He jumped up (he must be hyper-active too, thought Käfer, and also badly medicated!), spoke exuberantly to the caller and ran gesticulating through the seated crowd to the other side of the roof garden. When he returned, he said a curt goodbye, not with-

---

1) German for beetle, bug, chafer

out kissing Sirlana (Käfer looked away again), and muttered something about an urgent appointment. Off he went.

Käfer reached for the spot on his shoulder blade that he could just reach with his hand – where his transponder chip was embedded.

3.

The *Biotopp!* was a small bistro in "Monsterfelde", only a few streets away from DURATEC. Now, in the late afternoon, it was rarely occupied. Lasis sat alone at the round table in the back, from where he could keep an eye on the entrance area. In front of him was his drink, a *Berliner Weiße* in the green version. In his hand he held his tablet PC, on which he had called up the latest edition of the daily newspaper.

As so often, he was annoyed with the device. Today the graphics were jammed, or more precisely, the 3D mode wasn't working. In two-dimensional representation, the images seemed quite featureless to him, without any reference to the viewer – as if they were cryptographs from an earlier century. Once again, he asked himself the same old questions that come up when dealing with computers: Is it the device? Is it the programme? Is it the transmission? Or the source, in this case the newspaper? Would it perhaps work again tomorrow as if nothing had happened? He shut the device down, then started it up again, loaded the newspaper once more – no chance. Frustrated, he turned off the tablet and put it in his briefcase.

There really wasn't much activity in the Biotopp!, unlike in other restaurants at the end of the working day, when many employees, mainly of male sex, quickly take a sip to arm themselves against the upcoming domestic cosiness. Not so in Monsterfelde. Most of the scientists who worked here were always and constantly under stress, even if it was only because they were impatiently waiting for the results of their experiments. For that very reason they did not want to be forced into a rigid time corset. They chose their working hours quite variably, some even preferred to work at night.

Lasis kept looking at the door. Guests dropped in and left again. Mainly younger, aspiring professionals came, some just for a sandwich or similar fast food. He finished his Berliner Weiße. Should he order another glass? He remembered the situation on the roof of the company building. Mejul with that pale guy, Bernd Käfer, the head of the Department for Basic Research and Long-term Monitoring. This guy was as dull and featureless as his work. Even ignoring him would be too much honour. And yet, somehow, she seemed to find something in him. After all, his own status was also not really sparkling. Head of the Pharmaceutical Department. In other words, the company's medicine cabinet. *A pill peddler!* Not exactly an outstanding springboard for a career. The others could at least produce themselves in the technical literature. But he? What on earth had possessed him to study pharmacy?

The door opened, and in came a face he knew. The other one recognised him too. It was Jeff Schröder, whom he had asked to meet today, a strong, reddish type of eco-yuppie. They knew each other from a training seminar for laboratory electronics, where they had had an animated lunch talk together. It was about this and that, mainly about the lecture on the instant sequencing of DNA they'd just heard. According to the speaker, the new technique required just ten minutes for the sequencing of a complete sample, thus being almost on the same level as a simple photocopy. Moreover, it could be done by low-skilled personnel. A breakthrough for criminology, medicine and insurance business, as well as for 'numerous other applications that we do not yet know about'. This opened the door for various speculations.

'Crazy,' Lasis had said. 'Now the health insurers will strictly demand a genetic test before signing a contract.'

'Maybe they'll put a time limit on the contracts and ask for the test again and again,' Schröder had continued the thought.

'Probably. And at some point someone will say it would be a tremendous cost saving if the genome sequences of all citizens were stored centrally.'

'Would that surprise you? But I'll tell you what: you should see how you can swim with this current.'

'There's quite a lot of filth, I'd say, drifting with this current…'

'I mean… how to take advantage of this development,' Schröder specified. 'There will be a tremendous demand for services now. Just the collection and management of the data… and almost anyone can do it.'

For Lasis, whose imagination was not the brightest, the thought nevertheless began to take root. 'Sure… that might be a chance… the early bird catches the worm!'

'Maybe we can continue this later,' Schröder had said when the next lecture began.

Was this "later" now? Lasis had to admit that he'd given little thought to the subject in the meantime but was still fascinated by the idea. A business of his own! Maybe small at first, with two or three employees, but… all these rapid advances in technology… what profit potential opening up! But you couldn't stand still, you'd have to keep your eyes open all the time…

He was only a 'pill peddler,' but precisely because he didn't have any fantasy, he dared to do it.

When Schröder sat down, he seemed different to Lasis. The composure he had shown during the past midday talk had disappeared, and his gestures seemed controlled or even tense. Well, a little strangeness is normal, thought Lasis, that's always the case when you want to continue a talk after several weeks. First, you have to find the thread again.

But the conversation stuck to general topics for a longer time: the weather, the company, Berlin affairs, and so on. After an hour, it seemed to Lasis that he had learned much less from Schröder than Schröder had from him. All he knew was that Schröder was single and had a lectureship in computer science, specialising in laboratory analysis, at the BTU, the Technical University of Cottbus.

It was only when the third green Weiße and the second cappuccino were on the table that Schröder loosened up and reported on a spectacular new development by the Institute of Physics and Chemistry at the BTU, namely an electron microscope with a holographic image output. He had witnessed an experiment in which a freshwater polyp, three millimetres large in Natura, had eaten a water flea, both hovering above the laboratory table. Only as a projection of the device, of course. The water flea was the size of a football, the polyp the same. Both were completely transparent, like ghosts or jellyfish. One could clearly see how the heart of the devoured crustacean was still twitching in the belly of the polyp. 'That was fantastic!' he rapsodised. 'Breathtaking! That could almost replace Sunday's crime time on TV!'

'And you said the other day that one should be involved in these developments,' Lasis finally got around to his topic.

'Of course! The markets are just crying out for new offers. You, as a pharmacist, you know all the junk they need for their biotechnology. And I can write programmes to control the laboratory equipment. That's a good basis, isn't it?'

Lasis looked at him with his big eyes under the wide brow ridges. The stranger's enthusiasm, pretending to be his close friend, almost frightened him. He took a sip of his Weiße. 'You think we could work together…'

'Yes, why not? That's an ideal combination, pharmacy and computer science. And it's not so common, there are hardly any pharmacists. And the ones you could find weren't interested in technology.'

'Hmmm…' Lasis had not thought that the fulfilment of his just budding desires would take shape so quickly.

'But one needs money,' he remarked. 'Start-up capital. Subsidies, loans. I know this from friends. You have to strip right down to your underwear if you want a gift. And then you're always obligated.'

'Exactly! The state, the banks – they don't give anything for free. Some want to see results, which they then boast about themselves as their own successes, others want their money back sooner than you think. Just the first steps, the applications, take months and years. As they say – I've seen horses in front of the pharmacy…'

'… vomiting. Yes, I know. But don't you worry about the pharmacy. It wasn't mine.

'Sorry. It just slipped out.'

'So what now?' asked Lasis.

'What do you mean, *what now*?'

'Where do we get our seed money, then?'

Schröder turned his mouth into a broad grin and looked through Lasis into the distance. 'I think I might have an idea about that.'

4.

'No, not here, please!' Sirlana, sitting on his lap, pushed Lasis away from her in a way that he could hardly take seriously, and buttoned up her blouse again. He sent her his most frustrated look, which, because of his particular physiognomy, seemed so frightening that it would have sent any other person running. But she was probably already used to that, and there was no one else in Sirlana's office who could have been driven away.

'Shall we see each other tonight?' she asked.

'What a question! There's a slight problem, though – I've already got a date.'

'Oh! That's why you wanted to get it done quickly here!'

'Nonsense. I'm meeting someone I know.'

'That important?'

'Yes, that important. I've already met him once today. He says he might have an interesting offer for me.'

'What, offer? A new job? You're not thinking of going somewhere else, are you?'

'No, of course not! I can't believe you're so suspicious! There are many ways to tinker with one's career. Maybe I'll just give a lecture? Or write an article?'

Sirlana slipped off his lap and went to her writing table. 'That's true, of course. But why do you need anyone else for that? The mysterious man in the dark?'

'He's not mysterious. And I only said *maybe*.'

At that moment, someone opened the door without knocking. It was Käfer, who recoiled noticeably at the sight of Lasis. Sirlana smoothed her blouse again quickly.

'Have you got the message, Sirlana? DT 3.4 is online! The upgrade has been approved!' This time it was he who ignored Lasis.

'That's great!' she rejoiced, and Lasis also forced himself to smile. 'How do you know?'

'I was just with Renemult. He told me. The method is now officially applicable. His secretary is working on a circular right now. Maybe it's already there.'

Sirlana woke her PC out of its deep sleep, and voilà! The email was one of seven new messages.

'So our friend from Africa will definitely benefit from the new procedure,' Lasis remarked.

'Exactly. He will only be hospitalised for four days and then can jet off to Swaziland again. The rest can be done by the doctors there,' Sirlana said.

'There are no more regular control visits to Berlin necessary,' Käfer added.

'That's a good occasion for a celebratory drink, isn't it?' asked Lasis.

'Yes, tomorrow, I heard.' Käfer had nothing at all against receptions if they were for the staff.

When the head of basic research had left off, Sirlana returned to the previous topic: 'We were with the mysterious man in the dark. The one who wants to make you that great offer.'

'Exactly. He is not mysterious, as I said. He wants to give me a freelance job, or something like that.'

'That means – we won't have time for each other any more.'

He shook his head gruffly. 'Why don't you come with me and see what it's all about? I have no secrets from you.'

'I can't; I have a date too.'

'Really. Who with?'

'With my family. They just get restless when they haven't seen me for a week.'

'Oh yes, the weak, helpless girl. I get it.'

'You can introduce yourself to my father sometime, if you like. He's waiting for it.'

'Have you told him about me?'

'Only the good stuff.'

'So nothing.'

'Almost.'

5.

Rainer Lasis wondered why they had chosen the Prenzlauer Berg district for its scenic flair when in the end they decided to meet in an Argentinian steakhouse. There was nothing special about the interior, and the Argentinean style was only recognisable from the wine list. Nevertheless, the place was quite well frequented. Lasis had the impression that there were mainly non-locals who perhaps wanted to enjoy the atmosphere of 'Prenzelberg', but then again preferred the old familiar. He was sure none of his colleagues would stray here. He sat there alone again, an untouched glass of Cabernet Sauvignon in front of him.

Suddenly, a middle-aged man with his hair combed back walked up to him. Lasis had not noticed him enter the room.

'Dr. Lasis?'

'That's me. I, uh… what can I do for you?'

'My name is Matyas Karlik. May I sit down?'

'I'm actually waiting for someone else.'

'For Dr. Schröder, I presume. Dr. Schröder has been delayed. He'll join us later.'

The stranger quickly hung his jacket over the back of the chair and took a seat opposite Lasis. He smiled at him with friendly blue eyes in a round face.

'Nice place here,' he remarked in his unmistakably Czech accent.

'Very nice. And so avant-garde,' Lasis agreed sarcastically.

Karlik eyed his counterpart while reaching for the menu.

'Food is quite good here,' he noted after a brief study.

Lasis also leafed through the menu, which offered more than fifty main dishes in addition to steaks. All convenience food, he thought, wondering if there was even a single person left in the 'kitchen' to operate the machines.

'Yeah, not bad,' he muttered. 'I think I'll have a small pepper steak.'

Lasis was not entirely comfortable with the whole affair, and it wasn't because of the steak, half of which he hadn't touched. The man obviously knew the place, and he had very plain tastes for a Czech. He wanted something from him, that much was clear.

'Let's get down to business, Rainer. May I call you Rainer? My name is Matyas. With upsilon. Matyas.' He raised his glass and made a toast to Lasis. 'You need money? How much?'

Lasis was speechless.

'Hey, it's not a problem. Schröder told me. You have a project together? Okay, wonderful!' He raised his glass again and drank it down. The waitress saw it and nodded.

Karlik leaned forward, staring at Lasis. He lowered his voice. 'That's wonderful, Rainer. You have a project, I have the money. How much?'

For goodness sake, since when was money not a problem? No matter how much you have, it is never enough. And no one ever gives it away. 'Money is always wonderful,' he answered. 'Give me just one euro and leave it at that.

The Czech shook with laughter. 'One euro! That's good! That's very good, haha.' Again he leaned forward and whispered, 'One million? Two million? Just tell me how much you need.'

Holy Madonna, Lasis was beginning to falter inside. This would help, no question about that. Whatever this project was that Karlik claimed he had.

'I don't have a financing plan yet. I can't tell you for sure.'

'Well, let's say two million will do. Is that good, Rainer?'

The waitress came with two new glasses of red wine. Karlik grabbed his and whispered: 'Well, Rainer, what do you think? Shall we toast to the two million? Come on!'

Lasis hesitantly raised his glass and toasted with Karlik – or whatever his name was. They fell silent, each one thinking on his own.

'Of course there are some formalities,' Karlik admitted.

'Aha! So there is!'

'No, no problem, no problem. You'd just have to fly to London and take out insurance. That's all.'

'Insurance?'

'Well, *credit default swap insurance*. That's quite normal. It's common in this kind of business.'

Lasis, who did not know what was usual in such business, raised his hand thoughtfully in front of his mouth. His eyes under his bushy eyebrows sparkled. 'It's just a loan?'

Karlik reached for his arm. 'No. No loan! You can keep the money! But seen from the outside... a loan looks a lot better. The bank will ask you where the money is from that you're putting into your account. It has to look like a loan!'

Lasis wondered if such a sum in his account would ever look like a loan, with no interest payment and no repayment. And that story with the loan default insurance! The whole thing stank like hell of money laundering. His company would go bust, and the worthy Mr Karlik or his backers would receive clean money from London. Yes, they would even have an interest in his business going bust.

'Where is Schröder?' he asked.

'Oh, I don't think he's coming.'

'What?'

'He said if he's not here by half past ten, he's not coming.'

Lasis looked at his watch. It was just before eleven.

The waitress behind the counter let one of her rare glances wander around the room. Lasis raised his hand and called out:

'May I pay, please!'

'No, wait!' Karlik gave the waitress a hand signal that it wasn't time yet.

'No credit! No credit! We'll do it the other way! Listen!'

Lasis let himself be won over.

'So. Listen. Look what I've got.' Karlik reached into his hip pocket and unearthed a mobile phone.

'Obviously a smartphone,' Lasis said.

'Right. A smartphone. It looks quite normal.'

'Can do more, though?'

'Right. Well spotted.' He put it on the table in front of Lasis, who grabbed it and looked at it carefully. He found the on button and pushed it. The phone prompted for an entry to identify the operator as the rightful owner.

'Press the green spot with your thumb,' Karlik said. Lasis did so, and the mobile phone reported 'wrong input'. Annoyed, he handed it back to Karlik. He did the same, and the device was ready for use. 'It reacts to your fingerprint,' he said.

'In this case, more to yours. Yes, quite good. But it's nothing special, I'd say.'

'Now watch this!' Karlik reached down to his folder, took out a tablet PC and put it on the table. 'First, let's check the phone's memory. You see – empty! Now we put it next to the tablet. That stays switched off. Maybe ten centimetres apart. And now on the mobile phone – here… and… wait, file location… and go!'

A green bar appeared on the display, pulsing blearily along, steadily increasing in length. It looked as if something was being copied here. Shortly afterwards, the device reported 'done'. Karlik opened the file, and a text appeared that Lasis knew. He felt his pulse race and stared at his counterpart as if he were dealing with Frankenstein himself.

'This is the work order for the *DURA technique first treatment*,' he stammered.

'I told you the phone is a little smarter than others.'

'But where did you get …'

'It's the DURA 3.1 version, totally out of date. You can copy that anywhere, I think they got it from the internet.'

'And a copy is here on the tablet?'

'Exactly. The tablet was off, and yet the phone downloaded the data from it. Through the air. Sucked it up. Sucked it in. Sniffed it down. I'm sure you know a better word.'

Lasis stared at the device, half alarmed, half fascinated.

'Factory espionage,' he whispered.

'That's a bit harsh. Let's say: Mobile phone forgotten at the workplace.'

6.

The morning sun shone into the meeting room, where Director Renemult had gathered his staff from the upper floor. The occasion had not been named, but it was clear to all what was at stake: The six company departments were to be introduced to the new duties triggered by the sudden approval of the DT-3.4 version. It was more about a psychological than a technical briefing. The team should be mentally welded together to guarantee the success of the first usage.

Five of the six department heads were seated around the large conference table, which was made up of six smaller desks. Sirlana had opened her notebook and gazed dreamily at Käfer, who was leaning back with closed eyes as if listening to an orchestral performance in his mind. Lasis gave himself the appearance of being busy by leafing through a stack of files. Müller, who despite his missing academic title was responsible for the internal administration of the company, was looking amiably in all directions, only outdone in this by the company's young and dynamic press spokesman, Dr. Sahik. When Renemult finally arrived, engrossed in conversation with Dr. Kevin Weinberg, the head of the therapy department – the most important unit in the whole company at the moment – it was time to start.

Renemult chaired the meeting. He was, as always, in his favoured role as a moral shepherd of his company. With a sonorous baritone voice, he praised the previous efforts of his employees, which in his opinion had, as he put it, 'still occult potential for improvement'. He did not forget to mention his own achievements, especially his successes with regard to the short approval procedure for DT-3.4, and once again issued the basic directives: compulsory attendance for the entire staff during the next five days, double occupancy of all required personnel functions, and likewise double provision of all required medicines and supplies. His staff were not unhappy to have such a boss at their disposal. Externally, he had a high reputation among important decision-makers, while internally he had more the significance of a club mascot.

During the following discussion, Sahik asked to speak. He was not only responsible for public relations but also for client acquisition and follow-up care, thus as well acting as a scapegoat for all the adversities that arose later in the therapy. 'I would like to emphasise the words of our boss and warn against negligent mistakes. Mr Mswati has committed himself to absolute secrecy regarding his DURATION and all details of the entire treatment process. But if mistakes happen, if unforeseen complications arise as a result, then we all know what to expect from such promises. I don't want to sound sexist now, but just think of his three favourite women. It won't really help if the chit-chat takes place far away in Swaziland.'

His words were met with general nodding of heads; everyone had unpleasant examples of the past in mind. That was precisely why they had worked so hard to eliminate these errors and develop version DT-3.4.

The novelty of version 3.4 was that the added substances, such as hormones and enzymes, including the crucially important telomerase, were better distributed in the body by stimulating cell communication. This solved a problem that had caused headaches several times in the past. Individual parts of the body had, for whatever reason – because of 'calcification', constriction or curvature of the capillaries – responded less well to the therapy than others, while the rest of the body remained young. To give an extreme example: the client had the face and belly of a baby, the hands and feet of an old man.

DT-3.4 was to avoid these side effects. The knowledge of how it did this was subject to strict secrecy. It lay encrypted in the infinite depths of the company's intranet, in the approval authority, in the patent office and in the minds of DURATEC employees. In this respect, the event did not bring anything technically new for the assembled leaders. Nevertheless, they found the evocation of team spirit quite gratifying.

After an hour the roll call was over, and the staff headed back to their workplaces. Sirlana looked briefly at Lasis.

'Are you all right? Have you got your medicine cocktail together? In duplicate?'

Lasis looked up from the desk, where he was still checking his files. 'Of course, all clear. There's nothing really new on the requisition list. Enzymes, hormones, cytokines, signalling proteins and so on, all that stuff. Just different quantities and mixing ratios.' He leaned back in anticipation of her kiss, which did not come.

Sirlana's gaze dropped to his desk, where the smartphone Lasis had received from Karlik was lying.

'You have a new phone?'

'Oh, nothing special.' She didn't miss how nervous he suddenly became. 'The old one hooked in 3D mode,' he explained quickly. 'And the battery was getting worse too. But this thing is really good, here, watch this!' He held up the device and took a 3D photo of her, which immediately appeared on the display: Sirlana as a small colourful bust in a spatial miniature world to which the smartphone was only a window frame. A small theatre stage, an aquarium.

'Wow,' Sirlana was overwhelmed. 'And if I call you, will you see me like this?'

'That depends on the quality of your phone. I can't receive any more than you transmit.'

'We'll test that issue in practise right now.' She leaned down against him and finally gave him the kiss that answered all questions.

*

That evening, Lasis met Käfer in the underground car park. 'Have you finished my order yet?' asked Käfer.

Lasis seemed caught off guard. 'I'm afraid the things haven't arrived yet.' It sounded like an excuse.

'Man, put the pressure on! Otherwise, I will have to call off our series of experiments. We've been waiting for two weeks!'

'One and a half!'

'Don't joke! You know what we're working on. And you see how quickly our knowledge is being syphoned off.'

'Bernd, calm down. How can I help it if our knowledge is being syphoned off?'

'It simply means we have to be fast. Faster than the suckers. Don't you get that?' Käfer wasn't sure if his irritation really stemmed from the delay in delivery or from the constant hanky-panky between Sirlana and Lasis, which hadn't escaped his notice.

'Come off it! The matter with Mswati clearly has priority now. Were you asleep during the session? Man, I'm doing all I can!'

'That's what I'm complaining about. That's just not good enough!' The argument had now reached a volume that allowed a good evaluation of the underground car park's suitability for a rock concert.

'I want to see the stuff in my office in three days. Otherwise, there will be trouble ahead!' Käfer was red-faced, seething with anger.

'I like you too,' Lasis said impassively, turning off in the other direction.

7.

The big day of DT-3.4's premiere approached and passed. Mswati had apparently come through the procedure well and was cultivating a boisterous recovery style on the ward, where he and his three wives were occupying an entire suite – a new version of 'rooming-in', so to speak.

The excitement among the staff had also returned to a normal level, although the next admission – and with it one of those inevitable receptions – was just around the corner...

Next evening, Weinberg's closer treatment team met in a nearby pub for a quick drink. Later they were joined by Sirlana and Lasis. Sirlana and Weinberg engaged in technical discussions about possible complications of the new treatment, but as the spirits rose, they realised these could easily be dissolved in alcohol. Lasis sat by taciturn and gloomy, as if he were in a completely different film.

He was brooding. He had the mobile phone, he had the job, he had the plan and he had the prospect of no less than two million euros. Just on the side! For half an hour's activity that could not even be called work! All right, a somewhat stressful activity, but so what? Beggars can't be choosers in times of need. Let's not be petty now. However, what he didn't have – or not yet – was a suitable timeline.

He had discussed the procedure with Karlik in detail. The core issue to the whole thing was that the masterminds in the back couldn't simply hack the desired files from the company's intranet, as this was completely separate from the normal internet. Access would only be possible if there was a bridge between the two systems – i.e., if a user was active on both networks at the same time. However, the company's end devices were set in such a way that this would lead to an immediate shutdown of the corresponding computer. Therefore, one had to tap into the intranet by hand – with this particular mobile phone, which was also able to send the data on immediately.

It was actually quite simple. Computer on, intranet on, enter the PIN, call up the file – suck it up, send it – done. It couldn't go wrong. Lasis nodded involuntarily to himself and grinned.

'Well, are you finally getting into the mood?', Sirlana interrupted his thoughts. 'What are you brooding about all the time?'

Lasis snapped out of his thoughts. 'Oh, nothing special. I'm just a little pissed off. That's all.'

'At me?'

It annoyed Lasis that she usually blamed herself for his moods. In a moment she would start to justify herself.

'No, of course not! At Käfer.'

'Käfer? How can you be mad at Käfer? He's sooo peaceful.' She raised her glass and clinked it against his.

'You don't know him very well. Käfer is a monster inside. You should stay away from him.'

'Beauty and the Beast, heehee.'

Suddenly Lasis had an idea. He would do it right away.

'Maybe you should take a taxi later. In your condition...'

'Why? Aren't we going together?' asked Sirlana, surprised.

'No, I think I'll go now. Don't take offence, but I'm just out of place here.'

8.

In Monsterfelde energy saving was not an issue. The streets and car parks were brightly lit by tall arc lamps. Some buildings were glowing dimly against the night sky thanks to their self-luminous paint. Even the asphalt of some pavements was painted with a luminescent colour, which gave the passers-by an eerie appearance as if walking on a flow of greenish lava. Lasis, the only pedestrian around, marched quickly. The DURATEC building, towering darkly except for a few bright windows, was not far from the pub.

A few bright windows – that was good. There were still some colleagues at work, so his visit wouldn't attract much attention. With his old mobile phone, which was programmed accordingly, he opened the main door. The lift was turned off overnight, so he took the stairs. He took care not to make any shuffling noises as he walked, but still his steps echoed treacherously loud in the emptiness of the rooms. Dim emergency lighting was on throughout the whole building, including the corridor on the first floor that led to his workplace. He knocked quietly on the doors of his department – no one there. Another press on the mobile phone opened the door to his office.

Suspiciously he looked around. A rather superfluous action, because who had access to his office at half past ten at night? That would have been even impossible during the day. He switched the ceiling light on and started his computer. Suddenly it occurred to him that he should not alert any sleeping dogs with his brightly shining window – scientists could be very active at night when they felt like exchanging ideas. That also applied to the security staff. No, he didn't need a big light. Instead, he switched on his desk lamp and bent its stem all the way down, so that the lamp came to rest just above the tabletop. Or no, he thought, even better, the light from the monitor there is quite enough. He switched the desk lamp off again.

The new mobile phone could be activated as planned with the press of a thumb. The computer, after entering Lasis's PIN, opened the way to the innermost part of the DURATEC intranet. However, he had to search for the files for a while. They were cryptically named, and his department was not exactly the one that often dealt with methodical questions. But finally he found the folder with the simple designation DT-3.4. Crazy! Here, of all places, is the data on display, he thought. But his sneery attitude vanished immediately: to his dismay, this folder was secured with its own password. He groaned and leaned back. That was probably the end of his action. How was he supposed to crack this code? Was it perhaps

Renemult's birthday? They wouldn't make it that easy. And besides, when was Renemult's birthday anyway?

Käfer looked up at the night sky. The DURATEC building was shrouded in darkness, except for three illuminated windows on the top floor, which belonged to the IZN. His department was one below, right next to Lasis's pharmacy. Käfer was driven by his ideas on rejuvenation, the old dream of mankind and the next upgrade of the DURA technique, and wanted to go through the documents on Coelenterates, the "hollow animals", again. Some of them, for example jellyfish, were known to be able to live forever, just like single-celled organisms, if they did not fall prey to the so-called 'catastrophic death', that is, if they were not eaten. But in the case of *Turritopsis dohrnii*, a completely ordinary-looking jellyfish, this ability went even further: it could also rejuvenate itself. It simply turned back into its juvenile stage, a sessile polyp, and started its life all over again. It was almost as if a butterfly didn't die but pressed the 'restart button' and simply changed back into a caterpillar.

As Käfer approached the building, he noticed that a light suddenly went on in the pharmacy, probably in Lasis's office. All right, he thought. I'll sneak past in the corridor. Or stop! Even better: I'll ask the guy for my order again. At least he can tell me what he has done so far. No sooner had he thought this than the light was extinguished again, or rather, it was replaced by a dull glow. Käfer stopped and peered. To his surprise, the light in the room swung wildly back and forth, then almost faded and finally went out completely.

This was somewhat strange. Was that really a member of the company up there? Was someone perhaps searching for drugs? He had read about several such break-ins recently. In any case, he should inform security and not go upstairs alone. Or stop! Was Lasis perhaps up there with Mejul? That was just like him. That could explain the light spectacle. It was none of his business, but... He would check for himself before calling security.

Meanwhile, Lasis entered the fifty-seventh password. He had written them all down and counted them. The computer hadn't been impressed by any of them, and Lasis wondered if at some point the access to the network would be completely denied. Then he had an idea: lacking imagination, many colleagues simply use the release date as their password. He could still try that. When was the last version of the DURARE technology finally completed? Renemult had mentioned the date at Mswati's reception, but Lasis couldn't remember it. Two months ago, perhaps. Then his eyes fell on a circular lying on his desk, and he found the date: it was 27.2.2047.

He typed it in, and the computer rejected it.

It was exasperating. Cursing softly, he buried his face in his hands. It wasn't meant to be. After all, it wasn't right what he was doing. He stared at the monitor as if he could simply think away the ‚access denied'. He tried it one last time and entered the numbers not with dots but with hyphens. Eureka! This time it worked! The documents on DT-3.4 spilled into the working memory. It was a pretty large file. It contained many pictures and graphs and was blown up to thirty-eight gigabytes. Not too big for his working memory, but easily too big for the smartphone. But he would see that in a moment.

He took it in his hand and weighed it carefully, as if he could feel that it was still "empty". Then he placed it just as solemnly on the processing unit which stood on the floor, and pressed ‚enter'. The 3D display flashed up and showed a transparent bar in a perfectly blue universe. Its left end began to pulse green. "Migrating Data" was emblazoned above it.

'Come, come to daddy…' Lasis was more than happy.

Käfer walked down the corridor and was still not sure if he should actually open Lasis's office door. He felt a little sick. If he needed the security, what should he do? Scream? Fumble out his mobile phone and call them? He stopped in front of Lasis's office and listened. What he heard seemed like someone humming 'We are the Champions, my Friend…' softly to himself. Then he took heart and pushed down the door handle without warning.

Rainer Lasis spun around as if he had choked on the melody. 'Oh, it's just you,' he stammered.

'Who did you think it was? A burglar?' Käfer felt mighty good to find his adversary so stunned, even if he could barely recognise him in the dark. 'Don't worry, that's what I also thought when I saw the lights twinkling from below. Why are you sitting in the dark? Doing some dark deeds, eh?' Grinning, he approached Lasis, who was frantically searching for an explanation.

'What are you doing here at this hour?' was the only thing that came to Lasis's mind.

'Me? Well, what are YOU doing here, that's the question, isn't it? As for me... I just wanted to ask you about my chemicals. My order, you remember?' At this, he bent down a little so that he could see what kind of file it was. Instinctively, Lasis let the starting menu pop up, covering everything else.

'Oh, top secret?'

It seemed to Lasis that his colleague was taking everything on the funny side, and he drew some hope. He wanted to turn over the mobile phone whose bar was pulsing treacherously, but Käfer's leg was right in front of it. He had to keep his colleague busy so he wouldn't look down, it flashed through his mind.

'Your pharmaceuticals... I traced the shipment on the computer. You'll have it tomorrow. Hey – wasn't there a noise outside?' He stood up in a flash and hurried to the door.

Käfer had heard nothing and remained standing, looking after him. Then he let his eyes, which by now had become accustomed to the darkness, roam over the desk, the lamp of which was drawn down so strangely. So that was the play of lights from before, he thought. Weird! And his obvious nervousness... Yes, if someone should be out there, it would most likely be the night watchman. Funny guy!

'Hey, is someone there?' Lasis yelled and hastily ran to the left, towards the entrance of the corridor.

That's when Käfer spotted it. The smartphone lying on the

processing unit, the transparent bar already half filled by the green pulsating finger. Spontaneously, he bent down and took it off the computer. Immediately a red warning message appeared: TRANSMISSION DISRUPTED - DEVICE DISCONNECTED.

Transmission disrupted? What was being transmitted here? He stared at the phone, then at the computer screen which was still showing the starting menu. On the task bar a little yellow icon attracted his attention. He moved the cursor to it and clicked on it. Out came a file he knew only too well.

'Oh shit!' he shouted. Suddenly it was clear to him what it was all about. 'Rainer! What the hell is this! Rainer, stop!' He turned, ran into the hallway and just saw Lasis open the door to the stairwell and disappear.

'Rainer!' Käfer yelled as loud as he could, 'Come back! There's no point in this!'

9.

There was an awkward silence in the meeting room. Even Renemult, who could seldom stop his flow of words, said nothing. He himself had called the crisis meeting for eight thirty, after Käfer had rung him out of bed during the night and reported what had happened. Klara Mundt, the chief secretary, had personally gone through the departments and rounded up their leaders; she only missed Mejul Sirlana. Nobody knew where she was. It was assumed that she had stayed in the hospital where Lasis had been admitted after the fight with the guard. After a quarter of an hour, Renemult heaved a deep sigh and opened the meeting.

Actually, everything was clear. The corpus delicti – the smartphone – had been confiscated by Käfer. The perpetrator was clearly identified and lay well guarded in the prison hospital. There were two observers, Bernd Käfer and the guard, who could clearly testify to the course of events. The criminal significance of what had happened was perfectly obvious. The motive of the perpetrator, however, was unclear. Had he been threatened? Blackmailed? Bribed? Lasis, who was entirely capable of answering questions, had so far remained silent.

Renemult made no secret of his disappointment at his colleague's failure. The others saw it the same way but were still amazed at how abrupt and total their boss's change of heart was. If he had recently praised Lasis for his reliable, not to say intelligent, logistics, he now put him in a light as if he had always been a shady character.

Probably, Käfer thought, he now sees himself under pressure to explain to the Charité, the Senate and the entire public why he did not have his institute under control. And he was certainly preparing his line of defence, implying that Lasis had always been an evil element that simply could not be tamed when collaborating with insidious, internationally controlled circles. Or no, that was precisely the wrong message if potential clients' trust in the firm was not to be damaged. Renemult was caught in the announcement trap. No matter what he said, it was wrong. Best, thought Käfer, to stick to the simple truth. He was curious to see what would happen next.

'The following is to be clarified from our side,' Renemult continued. 'Are the data transmitted to the criminals very important? Therefore we need the technical report from the police. Maybe it wasn't that tremendous. Secondly, how can we protect ourselves from similar attacks in the future? Perhaps there is only one way: to print the important files out and store the sheets in the safe at Mrs Mundt's. Or we will install an external memory there. However, if one of our own team…' He looked around, general suspicion sparkling in his eyes. 'Unfortunately, progress is not only on the side of the good guys.'

'Well, the way I interpret the smartphone display…' Käfer interjected. 'The copy of the file is obviously to a great extent incomplete. Maybe the radio transmission to the backers was actually simultaneous, but even then it only happened partially. I'm quite optimistic about that.'

'We'll see,' said Renemult, 'if somewhere in the East an institute starts to promote the new method – under a different name, of course – then it will probably have worked. Those guys plagiarise everything regardlessly!'

'Why only in the East?' asked Sahik, who, for whatever reason, could afford to object.

'Why? Oh yes, what I wanted to say: We are opening a branch in the States soon. Didn't I mention that? No? Well, now you know.'

A murmur went through the group, alternating between agreement and dismay.

'Things are different between friends. You know that, don't you?' With these words, Renemult closed the meeting and set the continuation for three o'clock in the afternoon.

On the way to his office, Käfer wondered where Sirlana was. Was she with Lasis? In any case, it was good that she hadn't been there. She would have protected her lover and easily provoked a quarrel with Renemult. Considering his mood today, it could have gone badly wrong.

10.

Sirlana was sitting at home at the kitchen table, staring out of the window. In front of her, four storeys below, flowed the Havel, which was very wide here. On it she saw the barges that evenly pulled their course from south to north, from north to south. If she let her gaze wander over the flat industrial buildings on the other bank and over the adjoining allotments, she could see the high-rise buildings of the BIOBIG in the background. Between them she could guess the location of DURATEC. It was actually a very beautiful area here in *Spandau-Neustadt*, at least by the standards of a metropolitan city. Not too far from her workplace, even if the public transport there was not the best.

Despite these pleasant impressions, she did not really notice what she saw. The unsettling news of the night's incident, which her colleagues had given her in the early morning, had shaken her badly. Of course, she had gone to the judicial hospital immediately. Fortunately, Lasis's injuries weren't half as serious as she had feared. A dislocated arm, some grazes on his face and slight concussion – nothing that would cause any permanent injury.

It was a different story, however, with the accusations made against him by their colleagues. According to them, Rainer Lasis was supposed to have spied out the latest version of their treatment concept and then immediately passed it on to dubious backers abroad – an almost impossible idea for Sirlana. Rainer, with whom she had been more or less firmly involved, who she had trusted and sometimes told operational details that were not actually meant for him – Rainer, whose physical presence touched her in such a way that she felt she was more, much much more than just an endless tangle of genetic information – a criminal? Her Rainer, with whom she had already worked out playful plans for the future? Who she possibly – she wasn't sure – loved?

In the distance, she saw the private jets of Berlin's business bosses take off and land. As she watched them, her feeling grew that she was possibly part of a hermetic network that connected her to the whole world. Often it seemed the planes would collide with the skyscrapers of the BIOBIG site, but moments later they appeared a little further on, unscathed in the blue of the sky.

Of course, she mused further, sometimes Rainer had been strangely distant. Several times – but these cases could be counted on one hand – he had kept silent when it would have been better to pour his heart out. Then she had not known at all what was going on in the black crevices of his soul. Once she had almost left him because of that.

But wasn't it like that with all males from time to time? Wasn't it typical for them to endlessly carry their problems around and want to find a solution on their own? Stupidly, she had once complained to Bernd Käfer about Rainer's stubbornness and what might be going on in him. 'Nothing,' he had answered. 'Nothing is going on in him.' For God's sake, he should know, he was a man! In any case, she had taken offence and avoided him for a while, even though she was sure he felt something for her. And that she was not uncomfortable about it.

It had been similar at the hospital this morning. Rainer had woken up around ten o'clock and at first seemed completely disoriented. His eyes had had a dull expression, and as the first thing he saw was her face, he seemed to conclude that he was in the bedroom at home. But when realising that he was in the hospital, he became completely upset. He straightened up and wanted to jump out of bed, but she held him back and gently pushed him down again. His reaction to her questions about what had happened the night before was complete incomprehension. Then, when the memory came back and it dawned on him that he must be in the prison hospital, he looked even more sinister than normal and lapsed into a stubborn silence. Only when she left did he open his mouth and call after her, 'Can you get me a good lawyer?'

She wondered what was going to happen next. Both with his professional career and with their relationship. Actually, it couldn't go on at all, that was obvious. He would be convicted, which would ruin him completely, at least financially, and he would never find a job in a leading position again. The best thing would be for him to disappear abroad if he was not in prison after the trial. Which, after all, would also make any future personal relationship absurd. If it hadn't already come to an end by then. For she couldn't simply dismiss such mental abysses, such schizophrenia – such deception by a loved one. Could anyone? Was it even possible in principle?

Her mobile phone rang. Käfer was calling. 'Where are you?' He sounded excited.

'At home,' she answered curtly.

'Are you all right? You sound so tired.'

'Yeah yeah, fine, I'm fine. What's the matter? Why are you calling?'

'Well, listen, we had a meeting this morning and you weren't there. Rene was a bit pissed off. Nobody knew where you were. You didn't sign out. We assumed you were with Lasis.'

'Correct guess.'

'And? How is he?'

'That's what I'd like to know. Physically, he seems to be doing quite well. Tell me, Bernd, do you understand?'

'Understand what?'

'That one can behave like that. You caught him, didn't you? Did he look like a criminal? Or could it all have been a big misunderstanding?'

Silence at the other end.

'Bernd?'

'I'm afraid not. It all looks perfectly clear. Unfortunately.'

After a moment's thought, he added, 'I'm sorry for you, really.'

She wondered why, but his words did her good. 'You reported the matter right away, didn't you? Behaved properly.'

Käfer didn't understand what she meant. 'I couldn't help it. The guard held Lasis down and called the police. It was all clear then. I had to inform Rene.'

'Right.' Another pause.

'Listen. There's a meeting this afternoon. High priority! We'd like to hear your opinion on the matter. If anyone can do anything for Lasis, it's you!'

She had no idea how this would be possible, but in the end she agreed.

11.

Her car was parked at the back of the block. A blue Chinese coupe, not the latest model and not a showpiece either, but still technically up to date. Using her mobile phone, she

opened the doors, got in and threw her handbag onto the passenger seat. The car was still on autopilot, and she did not
intend to change that. On the whole, it was her experience that
the car managed quite well in Berlin without any intervention from the driver. She only had to enter the destination,
just as she'd done with former navigation devices, and off she
went. The pilot steered with the help of the satellites and the
server, which provided the latest updates each day at the first
start.

The journey to DURATEC usually took less than fifteen
minutes. Sirlana pressed the start button, leaned back, and
the electric motor started quietly. The car uncoupled from the
charging unit and rolled out of the parking space. It stopped at
Neuendorfer Straße, detected a gap in the flowing traffic and
turned south towards *Spandau City Centre*. She had to circle
around *Falkenseer Platz* to make her way across the Havel
Bridge to the BIOBIG. While her stomach was preparing for a
long left turn, the car suddenly steered to the right and accelerated in the opposite direction. At the same time, there was a
loud click in the doors: The car was locked.

Sirlana was confused. had she entered the wrong destination? Had the machine misunderstood her voice input? She
looked around and saw the signposts with the words *Falkensee*. Above it the blue symbol for the motorway.

Gradually, she got seized by panic. Her stomach cramped,
but she forced herself to think calmly. She pressed the button
for new destination and called out loud and clear: 'Yamanaka
Street One', the address of her workplace. Nothing happened,
the car moved on westwards, undeterred. Even after repeating
the procedure nothing happened. Okay, she thought, option
two: her mobile phone. She dug it out of her pocket and di-
alled the number of Käfer's desk. No connection. The mobile
was obviously working, but no call went out and no voicemail
answered.

Her thoughts began to spin in circles. What was going on
here? Was all the digital equipment down? The radio com-

munication interrupted? Was the car about to go berserk and, with an elegant swerve, crash into the next avenue tree? Another car was approaching; she waved her arms frantically and made all kinds of signs, but the driver, quite relaxed, just looked up from his e-reader and cordially waved back.

Scientist! Think logically! What other possibility is there? Ah, drive yourself, she remembered, turn off the autopilot. When had she last done it? It was a very long time ago, she wasn't even sure if she could do it anymore. Indecisively, she pulled at the paddle-shaped steering module, which immediately transferred the autopilot to standby mode. That is, *was supposed to transfer*, because no matter how much she jerked and tugged, it would not release from the dashboard, where it was embedded during the automatic driving mode.

While she was trying to do all this in a wild panic, the car had already reached Falkensee. At the fork in the town centre, it followed the priority road to the right and headed north-west towards Slip Road 28 to the *Western Berlin Ring*. Sirlana now signalled to every oncoming car, screaming in desperation, but even the crawlers being overtaken by her own car – imagine that! – only waved back casually, if at all. It was all completely pointless. Arriving at the motorway, the speed was reduced, the car took the first slip road and merged into the flowing traffic in the direction of the big *Havelland Junction*.

Where was it going? She looked at the charge display. The batteries were still almost full; their range at this speed was a good 350 kilometres. That was enough to get to Hamburg or even a long way into Poland without any problems. She now refrained from all attempts to escape her situation, because one thing seemed pretty clear to her: the car was controlled from outside. Someone had hacked into its electronics, presumably via the server connection, and was now using all the systems to direct her to an unknown destination. The person in question was probably sitting cosily at his desk, drinking coffee while checking her driving data on the monitor. How comfortable! Never again would she get into an automatic car!

She felt her pulse, racing but weak, and cold sweat trickled down her forehead. On the *Northern Berlin Ring*, shortly after Exit 30 *Schwante*, she fainted.

12.

A normal working day was out of the question at DU-RATEC. The scene of the crime had been sealed off by the police, which the security guard had called the same night. The officers had been swarming through the company since late morning, questioning all the employees, right down to the cleaning staff, confiscating files, and especially taking Penata, an administrator of the company's intranet, to task. Again and again, he had to explain the individual components of the system, especially the security precautions, and give his theory about the attempted data theft. Käfer had also been interrogated several times. To his growing concern, he realised that the police also seemed to be pursuing an almost absurd hypothesis – although the officer vigorously denied this – that he, Käfer, could also be the perpetrator.

It couldn't be more insane, he thought. Weren't the facts absolutely obvious? There was a person who behaved like a typical criminal by escaping from the scene of the crime; there were two witnesses who caught him red-handed, and there was the mobile phone as corpus delicti. And there were some other indications, such as the opened file and the hacked password. Of course, as a scientist, he knew only too well that one should not be blinded by the all-too-obvious! From that point of view, it was surely commendable if the officials did not only investigate in one direction. Nevertheless, when he imagined the bureaucrats at their desks who ultimately set the course of the investigations, he felt uncomfortable. Bureaucrats who were perhaps under completely different constraints than giving first priority to the truth... Fortunately, Renemult seemed to vehemently reject suspicions of any kind against employees of his company.

As the meeting was supposed to start punctually at three p.m., Käfer was the first to notice that Mejul Sirlana was not present. Renemult gave her five more minutes, then he opened the meeting. He said that they were to hurry because the police had scheduled further interviews for four p.m. Then he outlined the state of affairs, which was not much different from the situation in the morning. The assumption that no data had been transmitted during the night's action had been confirmed rather than refuted by the investigations so far. Nevertheless, the damage to the company was immense. The fact that Sirlana did not show up for the meeting, although Käfer had informed her, was strange in this context but, on the other hand, perhaps understandable. Everyone knew about her private relations with the alleged perpetrator.

Alleged. What is alleged about it, thought Käfer.

Then Renemult asked him to describe the course of events again in detail. 'How did it start? You had an argument with Lasis before? What was it about?'

Käfer described the cause of the quarrel, namely Lasis's negligence in the delivery of urgently needed chemicals, which had annoyed him. He had wanted to exert little pressure, nothing more.

And what drove him to the DURATEC premises in the middle of the night? Well, his future line of research, rejuvenation. He had an idea of how the abilities of the jellyfish Turritopsis could perhaps be used for humans. This was quite normal behaviour, which other colleagues also show from time to time. Wasn't that exactly what the phone app for door opening was meant for?

The silence in the group could almost be cut with a knife. Renemult looked at him sharply. 'One would think so. But it could as well have been the other way around.'

'How the other way around?'

'Lasis vehemently claims to have caught you stealing the data.'

'Wha-what?' He couldn't believe it. This was absolutely crazy! He felt like he had been hit over the head. Renemult actually thought it was possible…

'Lasis says he wanted to check again to see if he could find something for your delivery. Then he discovered you on his computer, copying the files onto this mobile phone. Since you immediately became violent, he fled and collided with the security guard. What do you say to that?'

Eight eyes looked at him expectantly.

'I'm at a loss for words.'

'At least your fingerprints are on the phone!'

'Yes, of course, I picked it up when it seemed so strange…' Renemult nodded in understanding. 'Sure, sure. But I'd be significantly more comfortable if they weren't on it…'

Käfer wanted to make an objection, but his boss looked at his watch. 'The further interrogations are about to begin. By the way, just so you know: The State Criminal Police Office has taken over the case because of its national importance. So you can tell them everything again. Bernd, they want to talk to you first.'

At that moment, the door of the conference room was pushed open and Miriam Semmler rushed in. She was the assistant of Klara Mundt, who was sitting in the room and taking the minutes. 'Professor,' she called excitedly, 'Professor, look what just came in!' In her hand she held a printout of a short email, which she handed to Renemult.

He took the sheet in both hands and studied it. His eyes grew larger and his face turned white. 'Holy shit!' he shouted. 'Sorry, folks, but our colleague has been kidnapped!' He passed the paper to Weinberg, who read haltingly:

> *Your colleague Sirlana is under our control. Send us the file DT-3.4, and nothing will happen to her. If you don't, she will die. You have until ten o'clock tonight. The address is info@lifetec123.by.*

A groan went through the room. No one spoke until Weinberg took the floor again. 'by,' he said, 'that stands for Belarus, I think.' Into the rising murmur he called out, 'No no, I don't think our colleague is there or on her way there. That's where the criminals are sitting, if at all. Sirlana may as well be trapped in a cellar around the corner.'

'Doesn't she have a mobile phone?' Müller, head of administration, asked.

'Right. And that can be traced, ' Renemult said. 'Ms Semmler, you have the number in the secretariat, right? Give it to the officers. And stay in the office, with the equipment!'

A systematic continuation of the meeting was out of the question. The interrogation appointments with the police, as they soon learned, had also been postponed for the time being.

13.

In the team of the remaining heads of department, everyone had an opinion about if at all and how the demands of the kidnappers should be met. That anything would be sent completely seemed out of the question. It also seemed obvious that the crooks would check the transmitted files before giving the signal for Sirlana's release. And it was equally clear that they would not wait until the successful outcome of the transmitted therapy instructions could be seen – that might be in fifty years. They would make their decision based on appearance. The whole thing just had to look like an upgrade of the outdated method.

Renemult was completely out of his depth to now take on the role of the strong man. He pleaded for a modified version that, as he put it, '… will immediately present these bastards with the bill.' He seemed to have no problem ignoring the fact that it was primarily the foreign patients who would suffer in the end. Käfer argued for the transmission of the original version, a statement that did not exactly have a positive effect on the suspicion against him. He also argued that the DT-3.5 version developed by his department would soon be launched anyway, so the hijackers would not enjoy the current release for long.

Salik was completely against any further contact with the blackmailers because a) they would not release Sirlana even after successful transmission, b) the damage to the clients' trust would be too great, and c) such a procedure would only arouse the desire of further criminals.

Weinberg recommended sending a slightly falsified file that would not cause any further damage.

Finally, Müller suggested a simulated transmission jam, which would simply serve to gain time.

*

Käfer met Müller in the gents. 'Your suggestion is the best,' he said. 'We should stall them. Perhaps in the meantime the police can find out who they are. In any case, it won't do any harm.'

'Or we could find Sirlana,' he replied. 'Maybe we can locate her.'

'I don't think that's likely. The first thing the perpetrators will do is take away and destroy her mobile phone.'

'Of course. But I have another idea. Shall we go to my department? We can discuss it there in private.'

Müller was the only one of the six department heads without a doctorate, and for some unknown reason he was on a family-name basis with all his colleagues, except his own IT people. They were openly calling him by his first name, Andreas or simply Andy. His office was a serene, well-structured place compared to Käfer's junk room. 'It doesn't look like this everywhere,' he admitted when he saw Käfer's astonished look. 'Just take a look at the EDP. They have only one principle of order there: the so-called "increasing entropy", in other words, rampant chaos. And only one kind of storage: constant sedimentation. But: Happy is he who recognises his limits. Even as a boss.'

They took a seat in the 'cosy corner' opposite the desk. The secretary, whose nervousness suggested that she was already fully informed via the grapevine, brought coffee and biscuits.

'What's this idea of yours?' Käfer asked.

Müller leaned back thoughtfully. 'All of us, you and I, we're DURATED, as they say.'

'Sure.'

'And our health data is constantly monitored, by means of a chip implanted in our shoulder. Ringing any bells now?'

There was a peaceful silence in Käfer's head.

Müller shook his head. 'I always thought Germany's brightest minds were gathered under this roof. But it seems I'm the only one who is at least moving in that direction. How does this control take place? I mean, by what means?'

'On the back of the electric beam,' said Käfer, who, it seemed, was slowly beginning to see the light.

'Bingo. By radio. And what networks are used for that?'

'The mobile phone networks.'

'That's right. I see there is still hope for the 'sapiens' that certain specimens of the genus Homo adorn themselves with. And by that, they can be located by normal mobile phone tracking. At least the radio cell!'

Käfer was completely perplexed that no one else had come up with this simple solution. Actually, everyone knew that the radio data of the transponders, which sat in the shoulders of the persons who had been DURATED, were collected by the EDP team and sent to the diagnostics department once a day in bundled form, or directly in the case of an alarm. Some of them even ended up with a staff member in Käfer's department, for statistical evaluation.

Käfer gave a tormented smile. 'So, let's report this to the police. There's no time to lose!'

'Take it easy!' Müller asked him to sit down again. 'The police, that's the LKA[2] at the moment. That would involve

---

2) Federal State Police. One level underneath the BKA, the highest police authority of Germany

higher-level, if not political motives flowing into the investigation. And where the LKA is, the BKA, the Federal Criminal Police Office, is not far away. And then maybe somewhere the Secret Service is also on the scene! Do you really believe that Sirlana would still play any role in this whole game?'

Käfer groaned. He had to agree with Müller.

'We have everything in the house,' he continued. 'What do you think happens if the values of one of your DURANTs deteriorate to such an extent that he faints, for example, and has to be treated immediately? He will be located by us. That's perfectly logical. However, it has never happened before.'

A ray of hope fell into Käfer's petrified brain. As if a fairy had touched his synapses with a magic wand, he could suddenly think clearly again. 'Of course!' he shouted. 'That's the solution! I can't believe I didn't think of it before!'

'Don't worry. The others should know it too, but so far no one has thought of it. Except for the IT people in charge, of course. I just called them. They're already on it, trying to track it down. Maybe they already have it.'

Käfer was speechless; he had rarely felt so much emotional confusion. And what would happen if they found Sirlana's whereabouts? He jumped up. 'Come on, let's go to your IT people!'

'Off to entropy, then,' Müller agreed.

*

The three basement rooms in which the central computers were housed, together with other equipment and staff, really did resemble a debris avalanche or terminal moraine, perhaps even a primordial soup in which new creatures were constantly developing from wires, chips and boards. In every room, as the human-machine interface, sat an IT expert or administrator who struggled (or at least appeared to struggle) to match the desires of company employees with the capabilities of the hardware, software and company networks he was in charge of.

One of them was Penata, the informal contact person of the group, a young, full-bearded man who, compared to his two colleagues, looked quite normal, even athletic in some ways. He was staring at one of his six large screens, each displaying something different.

'Have you got anything yet?' asked Müller. Penata showed no reaction.

'I mean the aerial photo you have there. Is that all in *Brandenburg*? It looks like the town of *Biesenthal*.'

'That's *Biesenthal*.'

Hmm, thought Käfer. He doesn't look like a nerd. But seems to be close to it.

'We've just had something.' Penata spoke in a low, steady voice. 'But the signal was completely buzzing. And only for a very short time. It looks like it came from here.' He pointed his finger at the screen, which showed a huge forest area. Müller and Käfer leaned forward and let their eyes roam searchingly over the treetops.

'In the forest?' muttered Käfer. 'Surely, hopefully they haven't thrown her into a hole in the ground.'

'Which would also be a hole in the radio transmission,' Penata remarked emotionlessly.

'Oh God!' Müller cried out, and Käfer's breathing quickened.

'We have to do something!' he shouted. 'Let's go. You can phone us when you've located the exact spot.'

He took a few steps towards the door. Müller hesitated, but then decided to follow him.

'There's something there,' Penata whispered. Immediately the two men were back at the screen. A red dot flashed in the forest not far from the *Biesenthal* city outskirts; Käfer estimated the distance at around two kilometres.

'Wait, I'll zoom in on the picture,' said the administrator and clicked the mouse. The flat image now became three-dimensional and gave the two visitors the dubious feeling that they were hovering above the treetops and could crash down at any moment. Now they could also make out some buildings and ruins between the trees around the flashing point. Without regard for the stomachs of his visitors, Penata moved the viewing angle back and forth, and in the spatial image representation one could see the different heights of the buildings. Of some only the foundation remained.

'The *Biesenthal* Bomb Shelter,' Müller said. 'It dates back to the Nazi era. That's where the ammunition for the Finow fighter planes was stored.'

'Bombs?' remarked Käfer nervously. 'First a hole in the ground, now bombs? What next?'

Penata brought the view even closer. Now the viewer's eye was suspended about fifteen metres above ground level and diagonally above a large, hall-like building with an office wing attached. It gave a derelict impression.

'She should be in here,' Müller noted.

'Let's go then,' Käfer called out. 'What are we waiting for?'

'You're not going to free Sirlana yourself, are you?' Müller shook his head in disbelief. 'Alone against a group of hard-boiled criminals? Possibly heavily armed?'

'Didn't you just say that the LKA was cooking its own soup?' retorted Käfer. 'Let me put it this way: at least let us be on the spot so we know what's happening!'

'We could be a little creative,' the administrator suggested. 'Not to say innovative!'

'What do you mean? What's the plan?' asked Müller.

'I'll come with you. Then you'll see.'

14.

Sirlana awoke on a hard surface and found that she was tied up. It was chilly in this gloomy room where she lay, chilly and damp, although it was the middle of June. All her limbs ached, and she felt a burning pain in her right calf. Nevertheless, she tried to sit up and look around. Opposite her, on a bench in the corner, sat a man whittling away at a stick. He had black, short-cropped hair, slightly Asian features and wore a dark leather jacket. A few metres away, to the right, squatted another man, who differed from the first only by his dark blond hair and central European face. He was playing nervously on his mobile phone. Both made an equally coarse impression on her.

'Look, our queen's awake,' the Asian said.

'I noticed that ages ago,' growled the Central European. Both had a strong accent. Because they didn't understand each other in their own languages, they spoke German. Or at least tried to.

Sirlana wanted to say something, but only now realised that the men had stuck her mouth together. She only managed to utter a short gasp.

'Well, queen, you want to say something? You don't need to say anything. Look, it's all right. Splendidly all right. You're safe with us, darling.'

The reply was an angry growl.

'Ooooh, you're mad? Needn't be angry. We didn't do anything. We got you out of your crazy car. You should be thanking us. Car was evil, not us. What do you think, Pavel?'

'I mean, you should shut your stupid mouth!'

'Heee! Powidl! Not like that, Powidl, not like that! You're not my boss!' He said it threateningly. Then he turned slowly back to Sirlana, who was lying on a concrete block against the wall. 'Look, isn't she beautiful? Dark red dress! I like that dress a lot. And what's underneath, haha.'

The presumed Czech with the nickname Powidl put his mobile phone in his jacket pocket. 'She's a stupid bitch. Aren't you? Are you a stupid research bitch? What are you researching?'

Sirlana looked at him with eyes widened in fear and shook her head.

'That's what I thought. Stupid stuff. Not for women. Could be something better. The way you're built!' His laugh was broad and bearish.

Sirlana jerked her bonds, screamed into the tape on her mouth and squirmed violently, which the two men seemed to enjoy with great satisfaction.

15.

The car, an open silver-grey convertible, almost flew over the country road. Penata was at the wheel and accelerated to over 120 kilometres per hour, which made his two passengers, who were only used to leisurely autopilot driving, fear they might be thrown out despite the seat belts. The administrator knew his way around Berlin just as well as he knew his way around the equipment dumps in his office and drove down side roads, the condition of which, however, was rather bad, shaking the car vigorously. (Was it a coincidence that the government of this federal state called its policy the '*Brandenburg Path*'?) Their destination was the former bomb site of Biesenthal, where during World War II the Nazis had stored their bombs to serve the military airport nearby.

The sun was shining, and it was warm. Under normal circumstances, this could have been a fun trip for three bachelors.

'It's now almost five,' Müller noted. 'When does the sun set?'

'After nine. Maybe half past,' Käfer replied.

'We have enough time till then. I assume that there is no electricity in these ruins, and therefore also no light. I don't feel like dueling with those guys in the dark. And that without a weapon, too.'

'Who said without a gun?' asked Penata, steering the car into a sharp right turn.

'Why?' asked Müller, startled. 'Do you have a gun with you? Do you have a gun licence?'

'Open my bag.'

The ominous black canvas bag, more like a pouch or backpack, had slipped from the back seat to the floor a few kilometres ago, making a rattling sound, the meaning of which Käfer had been wondering about ever since. He unzipped the backpack, and the first thing he took out was a large torch. Müller felt relieved. Then he reached in again and produced a black thing that looked like a large toy gun. In clear writing it said: ONLY FOR ANIMAL DEFENCE!

'What's that? A water gun?' he asked.

'Sure, a water gun. But for special water!'

'Vodka,' Müller said. 'We splash them until they're drunk. That would make perfect sense!'

'I'll explain,' Penata said, slowing down to ninety kilometres per hour. 'So, in this thing are cartridges with a gelled liquid. Clear?'

'Clear.'

'And this gel contains metallic powder! This powder will be charged with a high voltage. If you get hit by the beam, you get an electric shock. Like at a wall socket.'

'I assume this is not for people with pacemakers?'

'Not at all. That's why it's only approved for animal control. Like pepper spray, for that matter.'

'But the pigs holding Sirlana captive are animals too,' Käfer objected.

'Not really animals… but they might have dogs with them,' Penata added. 'Vicious dogs that you have to keep at a distance.'

'Exactly,' said Käfer. 'By the way, do you have another one of these?'

After a short while they reached *Wandlitz*, which they passed on the right, and turned east towards *Lanke* and *Biesenthal*. There they took the country road 200 for a few hundred metres in the direction of *Eberswalde* until they came to a turning into an avenue. That led them through fields and a narrow strip of forest almost due north. At a quarter past five they reached the bomb site.

16.

'Can you explain that to me?' asked 'Beshbarmak'. That's what the Czech called the Asian with reference to a Kazakh national dish as revenge for the 'Powidl'. 'They were supposed to be here shortly after four. Now it's half past five. I'll tell you one thing: they're not coming.'

Powidl paced up and down nervously. 'If they ditch us…' He peered at the pistol he was cradling in his left hand.

'We should have her right now…' Beshbarmak looked eagerly over at Sirlana, who, judging by her apathetic expression, had resigned herself to her fate. His accomplice interrupted his pacing and spat to the side.

'What – we should have her right now …?'

'Well, you know …'. He made a thumbs-up gesture like a hitch hiker at the motorway. Perhaps a little more violently.

Powidl grinned. 'Good idea. I didn't think you had it in you, you bastard. What do you say, queen, want to have a nice evening? Shall we shorten the wait a bit?' He took two steps towards her and bent down to look her in the eye. She held hers tightly closed and turned her face away with a groan. Now came what she had been afraid of all along.

'Hey, we have to untie her!' said Beshbarmak and began to loosen the rope that held her legs together.

Powidl slapped Beshbarmak's hands roughly. 'Don't touch her! We must deliver her in one piece! Unhurt, do you hear? She's not going to a brothel. She's going to an institute! She's a researcher, if you know what that is! She's a researcher doing research works. In a scientific institute!'

Sirlana's eyes widened. She didn't understand anything now. A new joke? Nothing was what it seemed.

Beshbarmak jumped up, clenching his fists. 'You plum jam3, you! Who accepted the job then? And why don't they come? Why don't you call them? I'm telling you, they're not coming! They've changed their minds! And we're sitting here… '

'Shut up!' Powidl scowled even more than he had been doing since the agreed deadline had expired. Was it perhaps possible that the DURATEC company had already handed over the data, and the kidnapping had been called off? That they were simply left here with the victim? On the other hand, he couldn't imagine that. If she was supposed to be doing research in Kazakhstan, at a nice little, if somewhat lonely, institute in the mountains, then surely they should go through with it now that one already had her. What you've got, you've got.

'We'll keep waiting!' he decided. But what also made the situation tough for him was that his trousers were also getting tight because he could hardly take his eyes off Sirlana. The little light that reached the room through a small window was getting noticeably dimmer, although it was still far from evening. Powidl looked out. The sun was no longer shining, dark clouds were piling up in the sky. He glanced at the mouldy ceiling, which had huge cracks. 'If it rains, it will be uncomfortable here,' he remarked.

'Then let's do it!' urged Beschbarmak, affirming with a thumb gesture. He reached for the shackles on her legs again. Powidl paced up and down like a tiger. A chirping noise stopped them in their tracks.

'A bird?' asked Beshbarmak.

'A mobile phone, you idiot. They've found us. Come on, we have to go!'

While the Asian was still pondering who it could possibly be that had found them, he grabbed Sirlana. He had been longing for that all along, though not in this way, but still. He swung her over his sturdy shoulder and followed Powidl, who had already run down the long corridor, securing their path on all sides with his pistol.

17.

This should be it, the man thought in a language we don't understand. Up ahead, the big building. He glanced at his navigation device, which was specially designed for outdoor activities. But which entrance? Unfortunately, his device did not tell him. He steered his heavy off-road vehicle in a semicircle across a shrubby courtyard covered with concrete paving. In the hundred years of their existence, the slabs had become considerably out of position. They shook the car violently, so that the passenger had to hold on to the handle. The car stopped in front of a disorderly mound of concrete slabs. While they were still getting their bearings, the two people they had arranged to meet came running out of a door, the taller one with the kidnapped woman over his shoulder. The newcomers opened the doors and got out of the car. It's working out after all, the driver thought with relief. But why the hurry?

18.

That damned mobile phone! The ring tone had caused a real commotion behind the wall. Apparently, the criminals had been tracked down and forced to flee. Müller gave chase, though rather hesitantly due to the lack of a weapon. Penata swarmed out to sneak around the square under cover of the bushes and crumbling walls. After all – he at least had something like a gun. Käfer finally answered the call, whispering so softly that the caller's voice seemed to him as if it were booming loudly through the building.

It was Renemult. He was horrified when he heard that the trio had started pursuing the gangsters. Stop everything immediately!' he shouted and explained that they had gone back and forth, consulted with the police, and come to the conclusion that the documents should be transmitted. Müller's IT group was supposed to do this, but Müller wasn't there. He had obviously switched off his mobile phone. And so on. In any case, the conclusion of the call was: stop all action! Käfer rang off and stormed down the corridor where Müller had disappeared. He found him in a small porch, watching the process outside in the square. He positioned himself on the other side of the paneless window.

The view he was offered was absolutely magnificent.

For a moment, he saw the two kidnappers with Sirlana running towards an off-road vehicle whose occupants were just getting out. The next moment a fireball shot up in front of the vehicle with a loud bang, dust and stones whirled through the air, a shock wave knocked the kidnappers over and threw them a few metres to the side. Stones smashed into the masonry where Müller and Käfer were crouching, with a loud clang also hitting the off-road vehicle. It tilted, balancing gracefully on two wheels for a few seconds, and then fell over. The next bang was only a hiss compared to the first: The car burst into flames.

'Wow!' they heard Penata say from the other side. 'What a bombastic water gun!'

Then he jumped out from behind a little wall and ran towards the spot where the pile had been before, but now a deep crater yawned. Müller and Käfer did the same.

19.

Käfer first looked at Sirlana, who lay unconscious and unnaturally bent on the ground. A shock-like tension had seized him; he felt numb and moved like a machine. He felt for her pulse, looked at her limbs, and came to the conclusion that her left arm was broken, but otherwise she wasn't injured as far as he could tell. He took his jacket, placed it under her head, and carefully laid her on her side.

The kidnappers had fared worse. One had had his head smashed by a piece of concrete, another was spitting blood, the third had been buried under the burning car, and the last was trying to leave the place with a limp. When Penata gave chase, the man shot but missed. Penata also wanted to shoot, but hesitated in view of the experience he'd just had. The man disappeared between walls and bushes.

'Hey! Has anyone called an ambulance?' asked Käfer. Müller showed his mobile phone and nodded.

'Do you hear that?' asked Penata, listening. 'Is that a police siren?'

'Already? They can't be here yet,' Müller grumbled, 'they're still sitting in the stand-by room filling out forms.'

The patrol cars approached, and soon the first one drove into the square. The officers jumped out of the car with their weapons drawn and immediately took aim at the three DURATEC people. When the mistake was cleared up, the policemen – in the meantime, two more cars had arrived at the premises – took care of the injured and called for a second ambulance, a casualty doctor and a hearse. Two of them took up pursuit of Powidl.

'How did you find us so quickly?' asked Müller.

'Ever heard of mobile phone tracking?' one of the officers replied flippantly.

'But still! It takes over an hour from Berlin …' Here he broke off. Of course! The people here were from Biesenthal. The Berliners had notified them. How stupid could one be! The ambulances arrived shortly afterwards.

20.

Käfer was sitting at a hospital bed in the Clinic for Trauma and Reconstructive Surgery at the Charité in Berlin. He was gazing devotedly at his pale colleague, the head of DURATEC's Diagnostic Department, Mejul Sirlana, a physician herself. The attending doctor had told him that she had survived the explosion relatively unscathed and that her injuries were mainly harmless. Externally, only the plastic cast on her left arm indicated a lesion. The damage to her lungs caused by the blast was somewhat more dramatic. But even that, according to the doctor, should be forgotten in a fortnight. Sirlana had been sleeping. Now she slowly woke up, yawned heartily and opened her eyes.

'Bernd!'

He took it as a joyful greeting. 'Mejul! How are you?'

'Hmm. Kind of rumpled. What happened?'

'Don't you remember?'

'I have no idea. All I remember is that I was terrified. And that someone carried me away. The man ran. And then... then I woke up here.'

'Well... there were a lot of things in between.' He plucked up courage and grabbed her hand. 'For example, a big explosion with quite a rock fall. You were incredibly lucky not to have been hit. One of your kidnappers had his face smashed in.'

'Is he dead?'

'He died in the square. Another was burned under the SUV. The other two are in hospital being questioned by the police.'

She shook her head. The whole thing made no sense to her. 'But the fact that I was kidnapped – I don't understand why.'

'Well, I don't understand it either. The police aren't saying anything. But I figure it's like this: Rainer was supposed to steal the data from DT-3.4 and pass it on to the masterminds, who are somewhere in the East. I assume that some dubious supplier of DURA technology in Central Asia wanted to download the latest version this way. After this failed, he came up with the following game: He had you kidnapped and blackmailed the company into sending him the data quite openly to an ominous email address. If this didn't work, he would have you as collateral. You would have had to slave away somewhere, let's say in the Caucasus or Altai Mountains, in a special clinic... well, maybe you would have made it big there...'

'The chance of a lifetime! I missed it because you got in the way! But no, I rather think I would have had to give some local lord some remedies that would only achieve one thing: nothing. The main thing is to get the dough from the rich. And – surprise, surprise – there are no unpleasant side effects. The fraud wouldn't become obvious for at least fifty years. Dead! Oh, yes, bad luck, there's always a bit of shrinkage. But you can still sue, haha.'

Käfer joined in her laughter, then twisted his face mischievously. 'So you think I'm just an obstacle in your path? There's nothing more to say?'

'Yes, there is, there's a lot more. For example: How did that bombastic explosion happen?'

'Oh, that's easy. Penata fired his super-trooper high-tech water pistol at the men getting out of the car. Somehow, he hit the pile of clay tiles, under which there was an old bomb... An old detonator and the high voltage from the ammunition came together, and – whoosh! The flying pieces of concrete did the rest.'

'Penata must have had quite a shock. I doubt he expected that.'

'No, and to be honest – somehow he still thinks it wasn't the bomb at all ...'

21.

'It's approved! DT-3.5 is online!' Käfer couldn't calm down at all. He ran down the corridor, ripped open all the doors, and shouted his message to his colleagues. He also opened Sirlana's door, rushed to her desk and gave her a kiss before she could do it herself and before the colleagues who now filled the corridor could witness. 'We can use the new procedure. Starting tomorrow!'

'Great!' she exclaimed, 'that was quick this time! Who would have thought it! Only seven months after DT-3.4!'

'Who's coming tomorrow?' All at once Käfer realised that another one of those hated receptions was due then.

'Oh, some cult leader. I've forgotten what he calls himself. Toutmosel or something.'

'And he doesn't want to go to heaven?'

'No, he says he has received instructions from God to continue to work towards the salvation of his flock and to endure on earth.'

'I don't think I'll join that sect for a while.'

'In any case, we'll celebrate first!'

'Exactly! During the lunch break! Klara is already ordering the champagne!'

'Are you bringing your jellyfish too?'

'Turri? Of course it can come. It's the main person, isn't it?'

'I can already see the picture in the newspaper,' a colleague intervened. 'Bernd out for a walk with Turry in a wheeled aquarium on a leash.'

'So, who's stealing the data this time?' Penata suddenly stood in the doorway.

Käfer grinned. 'Hey, you of course, you old grouch!'

'Why me?'

'Because then you can play the great saviour again! But don't forget the water pistol!'

IV

Zeus is Telling a Joke

Zeus's jokes aren't what they used to be. Especially lately, when he looks somewhat decrepit, his bon mots seem a bit forced, and no one is blown away anymore.

'Do you know this one?' he asks the audience. 'Three gods got lost in a spiral nebula. They are… wait a minute… Huitzi Huitzi…'

'Huitzilopochtli,' Athena helps him. 'Isn't that a difficult name, Papa?'

'Yes, dear, it is. So Pochtli, then Jahweh and that Vishnu. The one with the four arms.'

The listeners know what's coming now, or rather, what should come, and can help Zeus with the punchline if necessary, in case he has forgotten it again.

'And where were they going?' asks Thor, who is also part of the chatgroup that has separated itself from the other gods. Several thousand of them have gathered here on Little Magellan's Cloud.

'They were on their way to this newly discovered Kepler planet. Just to check if they could create something new there.'

'628 f,' Athena says.

'Hmm… Kepler 628 f. Numbers aren't really my thing,' grumbles Zeus.

'Usually nothing comes of it,' Enki, the old Sumerian, has his say. 'At least as far as intellectual life is concerned. Either it doesn't work because the environmental conditions are unfavourable, or the eggheads kill each other as soon as they're created.' His fellow gods nod sadly.

'So, the three in the nebula. What happened then?' asks Ares, who has appeared in full armour as usual, stepping from one foot to the other.

'Pochtli said, "Let's keep walking straight ahead, the soup has to end sometime."'

'Well spotted!' As a god of war, Ares knows all about battle plans. 'Cheerfully going forward is usually best.'

Zeus shakes his head. 'Yahweh said, ,Let's go back and bypass the murky broth. We have only just got into it, after all.''

'Tinnef!' protests Yahweh, sitting off to the side, but without taking his eyes off the lumps of clay he has laid out on a board. 'I am the creator god! The sole one, by the way. I would have created the mess away!'

His colleagues ignore the affront. They've grown accustomed to his outbursts over eons. He will never change, the almighties can try as hard as they like to convince him that he's wrong.

'And what did I say?' Vishnu stretches out his four arms questioningly, making him appear (along with his two legs) like an insect.

'Yes… that's the joke. You said… er, because you said…' Zeus really can't tell jokes anymore. Now he has forgotten the punch line again! He searches his mind desperately, but he can't think of it. It didn't use to be like that at all. When you think of his Giant-jokes or those raunchy transformation jokes… for example with the boar and the virgin… The roaring laughter from back then is only a faint memory. In general, there is not much going on with him anymore. This also applies to the other gods, who seem to have somehow lost their divine spark in the last centuries. Let's be honest: As listless and grizzled as they sit around here, struggling for a little cheerfulness – who would still sacrifice a sick rabbit for them? But what is the reason? Has the nectar gone bad? The mead? Or the ambrosia?

'We're out of ambrosia,' Behemoth shouts across the space, drowning out the background murmur that people mistakenly associate with the Big Bang but is actually the murmur of the gods.

'Me too!' Zeus shouts, raising his empty glass.

'Fool!' scolds his wife Hera. 'I's run out! Not: lots of ambrosia! What on earth is the matter with you?'

'And nectar?' insists Zeus.

'Nectar spritzer is still there. Saved especially for you,' says Behemoth, who has stepped in unnoticed and keeps changing his shape, so that he looks like a rhinoceros one moment, then more like Lucifer the next.

'And where does the water come from? From the earth? Or did you piss in it again?' Zeus shakes himself. 'Nah, thanks, no need.'

Suddenly there is movement in the crowd of gods. It is an awe-inspiring sight. As if on a secret command, the surroundings, which are unique for each god and, of course, also for the author and reader of these lines, begin to trickle away, the deities float in nothingness or in space interwoven with colourful strings, to gradually gather like iron filings between the poles or arms of snow crystals around a midpoint, and finally condense into an arrangement that resembles a hemisphere open at the side. In the centre of this imaginary sphere one sees, at first completely transparent, then becoming more and more corporeal, a shimmering nucleus that flickers and swells and takes shape until one recognises what or who it is. It is Thot, the god of science, recognisable by his long ibis beak that sticks out like a spike from the black Frank Zappa mane.

While the ancient Egyptian leisurely looks around, we see the black horn-rimmed glasses he has never worn before (can you imagine a god with defective vision?). They are supposed to give him an imposing appearance, on this momentous day of his, but his pose seems rather arrogant, a little ridiculous. The fact that he, like the others, does not look particularly well also contributes to this impression. Even the pompous materialisation (he could have just as well come on foot) doesn't go as smoothly as he would have liked: Thot flickers precariously, even disappears again completely several times.

Zeus had consulted his family doctor Asclepius because of his indisposition, who had squirmed a lot and hadn't really wanted to come clean with his diagnosis. In addition, he looked a bit tired himself, one could have thought he was suffering from the same illness as Zeus. But in the conversation with the healer, it at least came out that almost all the gods showed similar symptoms. Were they perhaps getting old? Or really sick? Would there soon be no more gods in the universe? The fact that some of them were still bursting with strength and drive spoke against this theory. Among them were the idio-syncratic Christian god Yahweh (aka Jehovah), his cousin Al-lah, who never took part in such gatherings (perhaps to avoid being infected?), Vishnu, Shiva, and all the other gods and goddesses with an Indian faith background. Strange!

When all the medicines and also the loving care of his wife Hera (also no longer as intense as before…) had no effect, Zeus came to the conclusion that it must be something bigger that affected everyone, possibly a pandaemic (Pan immediate-ly denied it), which had to be clarified within the framework of an intercosmic study. He called together the small council of the gods, which commissioned a corresponding study. The contractor was the renowned office of the said science god Thot. Humans might call it "Thot Consulting, THOCO".

Thot is finally stable in the middle of the circle and has tak-en up his position behind the hastily appointed lectern. In his hand he holds a device that might be called a tablet PC on Earth, were it not rolled up like a papyrus according to ancient Egyptian custom. While he tries to smooth out the unruly part, which he finally succeeds in doing, the members of his team take their seats around him. Despite their divinity (?), hardly anyone knows their names: Kriskas, Palavi, Sovij, Austeja, Marx, Einstein… They share the fate of all those who do the real work.

'Dear goddesses, dear gods, dear other higher beings.' Thot begins carefully, so as not to leave anyone out. Then he ex-plains in detail what led to his mission and with how much diligence and meticulousness they tackled the imposing task. Many questions had only arisen during the work, which had caused a not inconsiderable extra effort, the separate remuneration for which still had to be discussed – and so on and so forth. As is usual with such studies, the actual work was preceded by a survey of the divine community, which confirmed what had already been suspected but also led to some surprising results.

It was surprising, for example, that gods who were not exactly known for their accommodating nature, such as Satan, Lucifer, Tuonetar and his wife, Osiris, Mot, Hun and Vucub Cane, to name but a few, also participated actively in the survey. This speaks for the importance of the study across all spheres of the gods. Incidentally, the response rate to the questionnaire was "very satisfactory" (one is already happy about small returns here); the evaluation was, of course, carried out anonymously – as far as this was possible in view of the omniscience of many participants.

'What did the survey produce?', Thot continues meaningfully, and the gods remain so silent that one thinks one can hear the gulping sounds of the black holes in the distance. But anyone who believes Thot will now tell them the result – or the results – is mistaken. Showmanship is now part of the trade, this is no different in infinite space than on the small boogey called earth. Thot describes in detail which hypotheses have been put forward and which have been discarded after lengthy processing, which groupings have been set up and which have been rearranged, which symptoms have been listed, and which opinions and proposed solutions on the part of the deities exist. The simplest questions were not the easiest. Who was allowed to take part in the questioning? Who is a god or goddess at all? Who is just a spirit? A saint? Angel? Demon? Troll? Can gods who no one in the entire cosmos believes in any more even be counted as such? 'Right there is the key!' he exclaims theatrically, flickering dangerously again. 'Let me sum it up like this.'

You wouldn't believe it – is there a result coming now? Half of the deities are already sleepily sunken in on themselves.

Even Zeus is only awake because of his wife Hera's rib jabs. Thot unfolds his tablet once more, which refuses to obey him, adjusts his glasses and scans the screen.

'Here we go,' he says finally. 'We gods never wanted it to be true. Yet it is.' He coughs meaningfully. 'We all suffer – to a greater or lesser extent, and I'm not excluding myself – from what's called CHRONIC-PROGREDIENT INFIDELIOSIS! CPI for short!'

'From what?' asks Dionysus, leaning on his large mead tankard. Quetzalcoatl, the feathered serpent, writhes incredibly slowly and menacingly on the spot, his piercing gaze directed threateningly at the speaker.

'Yes, dear fellow gods, it is CPI, also called THEOLYSE SYNDROME.'

'Aha, now I get it.' Dionysus shakes his head, while Quetzalcoatl slumps back thoughtfully.

The wading bird Thot nods. 'We have been observing isolated cases for quite a while, but only now – also as a result of the questioning – is everything rhyming into a coherent picture. It is indeed what the vernacular, in its disrespectful way, calls INSIDIOUS DIVINE SHRINKAGE or META-PHYSICAL FAINTDECAY!' He looks up to the right, where the Germanic Asgard fraction has taken up residence. 'Not to be confused with Twilight of the Gods, my dear Odin. Unfortunately, you have already hijacked the term for your own purposes. It would describe the events here quite well. A gradual fading into the darkness. There won't be such a furious exit as you imagine. We will simply become paler and more transparent over time until we are completely gone. It's sad, but ...' Here, his voice fails him. He lowers his beak and stares at the electronic wrap on the console.

A faint, murmuring moan ripples through the divine hemisphere, which now already seems a little patchy and translucent.

'Not me!' shouts Jahweh into the round.

'Why, you don't see...'

'No. I exist, and I will always exist!'

Indeed, Yahweh, as we have already mentioned, looks quite fresh. Even Allah, who is not present (or is he? There is no picture of him, no one knows what he looks like), enjoys downright youthful vitality. And the Hindu gods – just another example – also seem to be doing splendidly. Just look at Shiva, who always has to dance because otherwise the whole cosmos collapses. It is a grotesque sight, by the way, to see him at the moment, in the face of such monstrous Thotic expositions, doing a jaunty tango with Paravati, his lovely partner, but he can't or mustn't do otherwise.

In addition to the relative vitality of some gods, various lesser spirits, who have hitherto eked out an existence as ugly demons, have suddenly attained divine maturity. Among them, not least Mammon, the former spirit of money and now the undisputed god of cashless payments and financial constructs – or rather financial crises, as many CPI-ridden1 whisper. And also a certain "Football God", actual name unknown. Remarkable and recently on the rise: God or Goddess (shall we say Godderess?) Gugel'Huu, seemingly sprung from nowhere. On the dark side, Terror has blossomed, which can only smile at the pranks of Lucifer, Satan and co. You can see: There are two sides to everything.

Yahweh's statement does not impress Thot. 'When I look at you like this, dear Jehovy – your beard is grey, your eyes pale – you too are ailing, I'll bet. You should pay a visit to Aesculap's practice and get the matter cleared up.'

Everyone in the room knows the nerd would never do that. His words provoke excited discussions in the audience, people look around curiously to see who is afflicted with the new disease and how much time this or that person has got left. Some remain bitterly silent, others get into open arguments with their neighbours.

'May I ask for silence!', Thor finally thunders. 'Private conversations outside, please! You can't hear a word the speaker is saying!'

Where in the cosmos is outside?

'... complicated explanatory model,' Thot is explaining. 'Please take it only as a hypothesis. We don't yet know how far it corresponds to reality. But at least it's a start!' He has managed to get the unruly tablet, which keeps trying to curl up, to lie flat again and waved around on it with his right middle finger. 'The obvious dwindling of our vitality points to a striking circumstance, namely that – please forgive me if I express this in such a scientifically sober way – we gods only exist to the extent that lower beings – humans, Borg, Vulcans, Frogs, Ewoks, Hutt, Na'vi, Yodas and a few others – believe in us. Believe to a degree that borders on knowledge. Or conviction, certainty, if you know what I mean.'

Surprisingly, a storm of indignation – as is not unusual with such questionings of one's own importance – does not break out. Is it because the gods are busy with other things, e.g. with dozing? Perhaps it is also because they themselves do not believe in anything and thus have an understanding for humanity and co – they are themselves atheists, so to speak. However, there are some who are investigating the possibility of an even higher being than themselves – who knows?

Nevertheless, Thot continues in his analysis: 'This increasing faith mistrust that is doing its rounds on the inhabited planets, this blatant confession deficit, or whatever we want to call it, obviously stems from the fact that the so-called spiritually endowed creatures – which we have created...'.

Thot and most other gods do not notice the eclatant contradiction in these words. So who created whom? Athena, Xiwangmu, the "Royal Mother of the West", and also Wen Chang shake their heads.

'... that we have allowed them to develop, I would like to say, more and more in the direction of intellectual hypertrophy – or, as some people say, "nonsensical wisdom". Let's take humans as an example! Wasn't it wonderful how peacefully and happily the first of their kind populated the Garden of Eden, with only good, truth and beauty in mind! Harmony everywhere! They didn't have to do any intellectual acrobatics, they were already complete – in their own way. Contentment and serenity in their gaze. A sensual and contemplative gliding through life. A single meditation. But then it suddenly ended. It began to go terribly wrong...'

It has to be said that this Thoth is not without rhetoric. Sure, at times he babbles pure divine gibberish, interspersed with scientific-sounding expressions. But then suddenly he formulates so grippingly that one could pass him off as a cosmic football reporter. He should hurry to finish his lecture before the death of the gods takes hold of him too.

'I don't quite understand – although I am omniscient, as everyone knows – why you are actually still here,' Jahweh speaks up in his tactful way (or what he considers to be). 'No one has believed in you for a good two millennia. Yet here you are, sprightly, leading the big talk.'

Thot nods silently. His staff look in all directions without seeing anyone. Only a few gods listen attentively, although Yahweh's objection affects them all fundamentally and existentially.

'I must confess,' Thot begins in a subdued tone, 'that there are different views on this. The most plausible one at the moment is the one that assumes a certain lag in the withdrawal of faith. This is due to the fact that creatures continue to believe in us unconsciously or in secret, although they have officially committed themselves to atheism. We are talking about deity-remanence. Of course it's not the same as before, but it's more than nothing. But one day... But let's stay on topic. The proliferation of mind in humans. Where does it come from? We have to be honest. From us! Some in our ranks simply can't control themselves and must keep on tampering with the creatures. Hey, let's see what happens. It's funny, isn't it? They beat each other with clubs, they shoot guns, throw bombs, burn each other with ray guns! Bravo! And the rest of us gods? Gazers! Onlookers, nothing more! Like at a traffic accident on the highway... er, yeah...'

As I said, it would have been interesting to know what it would have been like if Thot had been reporting a football World Cup ("Goal! Goal! Gooooaaal!!! We are World Champion!").

Thot: 'I'm only mentioning Satan, the evil serpent, as an example. Is he here by any chance? No? So, the thing with the apple. Did he have to drag Eve into it? And Prometheus, not here either? The one who brought fire to mankind and a few other useful things? At least he was called to account, as you know – the chaining to the rock and the eagle that ate his liver every day. An appropriate punishment, I think, especially in the light of current events. And some others of us, I don't exclude myself, have given them the script system, after all. Mea culpa! Ashes on my head!

But now it has happened. Every man thinks he is smarter than the other! That he is in the right and the other is not! That the thing belongs to him that another has. That he doesn't need a god above him, because what we gods used to do for him is now done quite elegantly by miraculous technology. Yes, many even flatly deny our existence, or at least consider any thought of us superfluous! You notice that I choose the masculine form – not without reason. So we have to ask ourselves whether human beings can even tolerate the level of intelligence that our colleagues and I have spread among them. Intelligence that floats freely. Intelligence that is not bound up in the essence of the creature, or, to put it another way: intelligence that is not held in check by religion.'

Thot's stirring words actually have the effect that most gods are now listening intently.

'But what should we do? I mean, we need an ideology as an explanatory model and a framework for action, something like a mental superstructure!' cries Karl Marx, no one knew how he got into the ranks of the gods. Yet despite – or because of? – his overgrown beard, he looks relatively robust. As does Buddha, by the way, who sits quietly in a corner of the room

114

and meditates. Presumably, they have simply been believed upwards to divine spheres by the masses – just like the gods in their entirety, as can be gathered from Thot's words.

'That exactly, my dear … What was the name again?'

'Marx. KARL Marx.'

'Aha. So, my dear Karl Marx, that is exactly the question now. What is to be done? There is only one answer to that: The creatures that are poorly endowed with intellect – as an example the humans – must be intellectually readjusted.'

'Meaning?', Quetzalcoatl and Huitzilopochtli huff unisono.

'Meaning: We have to dampen their intelligence. Or, so that even the last one understands: We have to dumb them down a little.'

'And the alternative is?' asks Satan, who had been hiding behind the feathered serpent and is now slowly creeping out.

'There is no alternative to this strategy. There is considerable constraint. The time is pressing. But, Coatl and Pochtli, the strategy does not only consist of de-rationalisation, as mentioned above, but rather we must put together a whole bundle of individual measures. This includes focusing people's psychological equipment a little on the sexual. While you fuck, you don't think. And we will surround all technology with a veil of magic. Nobody understands how their mobile phones work. In the eyes of most people, it's just a brilliant magic bone. We just need to strengthen that a bit.'

'I have an objection.' A small god, no bigger than a thumb, speaks up in a thin voice.

'Name?'

'Lem. Stanislav Lem. I'm new here.'

'Yes, Stanislav Lem. What's the objection?'

'Yes, well. People do, after all, work on robots, machines that do their work for them. A special kind of robots are androids, replica humans, if you like. As I have convincingly, I hope, presented in my Robot Tales (oh God, a writer, thinks Thot), there comes a threshold in this technology where these androids – or simply "droids", as some say – not to be confused with the "druids" of this Asterix... I had an interesting and also inspiring one with Teutates the other day...'

'Please, Stanislav Lem, what threshold? What do you want to get at? In a nutshell?'

'Yes, the threshold. At a certain level of complexity, these androids are able to reproduce themselves. Not only that, they can also evolve. To a higher form of existence. There is also a film: War of the... War...'

'The Clone Wars.'

'How? It's possible... There are lots of droids of all shapes. With widely varying characteristics. And there are other droids with remnants of human tissue, mostly cerebral in origin, again in all sizes and colours.'

'Globalisation rules the planet, just as universalisation does here, by the way. A nice approach, moreover, for our strategy of de-rationing. Everyone is equal, and everyone is special. Ha!'

'Well, I'm not finished yet. So once the androids get to that point, there's a danger they'll do away with humans.'

'What's the problem?'

'Then who still believes in gods?'

'Huh?' Thot is, as they say, left spitting.

'Well, I can't imagine the machines will plug in a faith app like that. What's in it for them?'

The gods, all wide awake now, visibly struggle for composure. Thot fixes his gaze on a red giant in the far reaches of the cosmos, as if he could solve the riddle. When he receives no answer, he murmurs: 'Isn't that just a matter of course?'

'Not at all! One could argue that the mind needs a framework, which religion provides. No understanding can get by without these... principle axioms. You can't try to explain everything. But, dear gods, with the androids simple taboos are sufficient, integrated into their software. ,That's the way it is, that's the way we've always done it, don't worry about it, just do it! Again, there is an interesting phenomenon: there are those who carry these taboos inside themselves and others who implant them… That's already two different ranks. Like, by the way, in Orson Welles's Animal Farm: All are equal, but some…'

'… are more equal than others. We know the story,' Thot grumbles.

'So again, who believes in us then?' Stanislav does not seem to doubt the attainment of a certain divinity on his part.

An embarrassing perplexity reigns in space, or at least on the Small Magellanic Cloud. All eyes are on Thot, who is struggling with his stubborn tablet and casting imploring sideways glances at his team, which is looking down at the ground. Zeus nervously plays with Aegis, his silver thunderbolt, Vishnu with his throwing disc Chakram, Thor throws his hammer up a little, which as usual falls down to him again. Shiva dances, but very slowly; his otherwise lively Tandava has turned into a kind of blues.

Then Thot is struck by lightning, and his countenance brightens. 'This is truly an extensive problem that Stani has raised. It was in no way part of the contract award. But it seems almost imperative to take into account the now recognisably more extensive problem situation and to consider a… uh… follow-up order. As it happens, my team could make the necessary capacities available at short notice…'

The gods gaze pensively into the infinite expanse where the red giant is making his preparations to explode; some nodding thoughtfully, others shaking their heads just as thoughtfully.

'I beg your pardon!' it shouts, almost roars from behind. The interjection comes from Wen Chang, who now hurries forward. He stands brazenly in front of Thot's platform and bows nobly on all sides. 'Wen Chang, most humble servant! As you deities know, responsible for culture and writing, and recently head of a newly founded Institute for Transcendental Strategies, ITS for short. Our team can also boast scientific competence, especially with regard to the questions mentioned. This would offer an alternative to the previous researcher, which … in view of the… well, disastrous performance of this… uh, company…'

Here Thot interrupts him: 'Honoured auditorium! I am completely unfamiliar with ITS…'

'Are you surprised?' chimes in Chang to the assembly.

'… The shop was obviously founded quite recently, perhaps only in the last few aeons. What kind of credentials does he have? What has Chang done so far? He has prompted students at their exams, slipped them cash notes, wandered on the Dao. Zero competence plus zero experience is…? What?'

Wen Chang turns to face Thot, who has stepped out from behind his desk and is waving his tablet violently as if to swat Chang away. Quetzalcoatl, the huge feathered serpent, slithers magically closer to the two of them, turning his head back and forth from one to the other with his pupils narrowed to vertical slits.

'You know how to define incompetence?' Chang calls out to the group with his arm raised. 'When fundamental issues, such as the existence of androids, are excluded from consideration of human evolution. What Thot has said about my person is pure speculation, but his failure is a fact!'

Before the two of them can start at each other, Zeus stands up laboriously, leaning on his thunderbolt, which he should be holding at the ready right now, and majestically looks around in all directions. Then he gazes at Thoth and asks:

'Where the hell is Prometheus?'

2.

Dr. Gustav Zehdenick was sitting in the laboratory of his small institute for gene therapy, staring sullenly at the profit and loss account for the past month. His pretty assistant Monika had slipped it under his nose with a smug grin, while he was engrossed in the latest article about the Methuselah Mouse Project. No, he didn't like these sorts of figures. Scientific columns of figures, statistics, evaluations – all fine, but not this ominous commercial number-crunching, where the results seemed to be solely the result of hypocritical reinterpretations and trickery. Depreciation, provisions, losses carried forward – that was not his world. His world was protein molecules, enzymes, pluripotent stem cells – everything that had to do with genetic engineering. And of course – Monika. Monika had already been a commercial trainee in the organisation where he had worked before. Even then, he hadn't been able to take his eyes off her, cute, strapping and sexy as she came down the corridor or balanced her tray in the canteen. Couldn't she do some commercial research in his office?

But she wanted nothing to do with him.

Even in the newly founded institute, she was unimpressed by his niceties, countered his innuendos as virtuously as she had balanced the tray in the previous company. Every time it got too much for her, she turned to Klaus Femor, his partner, who was happy to play the game. Gustav could have raged with jealousy. Couldn't the woman get involved with her boss like any proper secretary! But instead… instead… was there even a man in her life?

The P&L figures were truly not uplifting. The business was now only sustained by a loan from the bank, which was linked to the condition of a monthly profit and loss account. Temporarily sustained, mind you. Everything depended on whether the gene sequencing line continued to run reasonably well. Nothing ambitious, nothing certain. Was it possible to manipulate the numbers so that they would find favour in the eyes of the bank? With a little number-crunching, see above? Monika. She would know how to deal with the mess.

Of course, he wasn't entirely innocent in this predicament. It was the usual thing. He quietly thought of himself as a gifted researcher, one who would one day shake the scientific and the trivial worlds with an incredible result. And then he would probably no longer have a problem with his wet dreams. Monika would see! If he still wanted her at all. Her nose was a little pointy after all.

In the real world, he frittered away his time on various projects, none of which he was really pushing ahead with. As a result, the turnover of his GustavLab GbR, Institute for Genetic Therapy, remained within confined limits.

To be more accurate, it had started like this: Gustav had abstracted a few laboratory mice at his former job, a renowned genetic research institute, and claimed to use them as a control group for another animal experiment. With these very cute black-spotted white animals, which Monika spontaneously called "Dalmatian mice" (how cute! Not the mice, Monika!), he secretly took part in the Methuselah Mouse Competition. The aim was to breed mice that would last as long as possible and beat the previous records. The plan was to later transfer the results to humans. At the moment, the bar was set at six and a half years, whereas the normal lifespan for mice was three. So seven years – that was the goal Gustav was aiming for. If only once in his life he'd be successful! First of all, he would be the undisputed hero, not only of the molecular biology experts, not just of the entire scientific community – but of the entire human race! Wow! Secondly, he would be the first to apply the findings to himself and could easily extend his life horizon to 200 years! Wow again! And what's more, you would see. Research did not stand still. And the third wow (that would almost be the most important one at the moment): Monika could hardly ignore him in the future. At least not if he made her the offer of the second wow. 200 years with Moni! Oh Moni! What orgiastic prospects…

But his plan didn't quite work out. The first mice died after only a few weeks. Too much telomerase? Too few stem cells? It was not good if the "comparison group" wasted away while the little animals, officially tortured with questionable substances, were having fun in their cages. So he had to proceed with restraint. As luck would have it, a man sat down at his table in the canteen he had never seen before. He was middle-aged, had a well-groomed beard and beautifully curled dark hair. His eyes were clear, his gaze friendly. He was dressed somewhat oddly in a kind of tunic over long white trousers. A shawl fell over his shoulder in equal folds. Strange guy! But one is used to a lot among scientists. If one was really good – and this one was really good, as it soon turned out – he could get away with a lot. He had moussaka with tzatziki on his tray and ambrosia for dessert.

'Everything all right?' he asked with wide eyes, as Gustav didn't stop staring at him.

He shook his head but said: 'Yeah, sure.'

The stranger's name was Melvil, he stated when asked. It remained unclear whether this was his first or last name. He was, he said, travelling around the institute on behalf of Oiran Consulting, and was to conduct a study of the company's operations.

Oh dear! TERMINATION, that's the word that comes to every employee's mind when hearing such harmless chatter. Gustav immediately switched to the highest diplomatic level, which means he hardly said anything. Or rather, he limited himself to asking questions.

'So it's about previously unused resources? Potential for development?' He deliberately avoided the word "savings potential". So did Melvil, who addressed neither and talked about "bundling requirements", "chief issue", "increasing efficiency".

'But this kind of survey,' Gustav grumbled past the chicken leg he was chewing on, 'requires a tremendous amount of expertise, doesn't it? I mean, if you want to judge them from the outside. The projects are very different. In fact, only the project manager ever knows.'

'Don't worry, Oiron-Consulting is not doing this for the first time. We have our empirical values there.'

Empirical values! So they wanted to rush the matter! Now the word T-E-R-M-I-N-A-T-I-O-N flashed red and implacable before Gustav's inner eye. These people didn't want to deal with the real problems of the company. They only wanted to conceal the arbitrariness of their rationalisation plan from the (remaining) staff. At that moment, his extra tours with the Dalmatian mice came to his mind. That was the last thing he needed now! He had to make them disappear as soon as possible. But how? The rooms throughout the institute were highly secured!

'You know, some researchers ride their own personal hobbyhorses,' Melvil continued. 'Doctoral theses, publications, post-doctoral theses are written under the edge of the lab desk – you don't get the idea. In your unit, it's still within reasonable limits, I've heard.'

Thank you. But still – away with the mice!

'Whereas' – Melvil raised his eyebrows in the middle and touched his nose with his index finger, giving his face an incredibly tragic expression – 'some of these extra tours are of a very high standard. Yes, sometimes one has the impression that the really important work is not done in the commercial project, but on the side! With heart and soul!'

Gustav's eyes shone. Was the someone in front of him really thinking outside the box? Or maybe even understanding the Methuselah Mouse competition? In any case, one had to remain cautious! He had finished eating, just like his counterpart, and picked up his tray. Standing up, he asked, 'When do you want to come over? You know, the test series take a lot of time…'

'Right away would be best! Let's take the minotaur… the bull by the horns!'

Holy shit! Right now? Could he perhaps quickly instruct his interns to throw a blanket over all those…?

Melvil walked in good spirits with Gustav to the dish drop. Then they made their way to the second floor, where Gustav's mice were nibbling on their special cheese.

3.

Half a year later. Gustav Zehdenick inspected his mice, which had gained a few millimetres in the last few months and looked quite well overall. None of them had died. At first, he had been very apprehensive when Melvil had arrived with the syringe and used it on a single animal. Gustav had never heard of this stuff, this cocktail called Nektarin. But there was nothing he could say. He was completely at Melvil's mercy with this illicit side project. On the other hand, his visitor seemed to have a credible interest in the experiment. 'I'd like to do it myself,' he'd said, 'but the work... you know...' Could one believe that? But what else could he do?

In any case, this first mouse had tolerated the injection well. Since he did not expect too much from his own experimental set-up, he finally injected all fifteen animals, which they all thanked with obvious well-being. Would it really work, then? Was it true what Melvil had told him? This dubious guy he meanwhile called a fellow researcher? Where did he get the brew he called nectarine? And why didn't he carry out the experiment on his own? Gustav had often asked himself these questions, but the sight of his beloved Dalmatinies had always pushed them off to the back of his mind. The crucial thing was that the guy wouldn't tell on him. But by the way – what about the organisational report? To Gustav's knowledge, not too much was happening. So far, only the lower ranks – house masters, kitchen staff, etc. – had been questioned. Did Melvil also have a little private project going on that kept him from working?

His only worry was that the success of his experiment would not become apparent until the end. That is, when the record of six and a half years of mouse life would be cracked.

4.

Three years later. The organisational report had indeed been completed. It had cost some researchers their jobs. They had been dismissed and then rehired – for a limited period and under worse conditions. Gustav Zehdenick had not been spared the same fate. However, he had refused the offer of a new job.

'Look at it this way,' Melvil had whispered to him. 'This is now a unique opportunity to start your own business. Imagine: No more interfering in your research! No more mouse experiments under covers! And once you've won the Methuselah Mouse Prize, the honour will be all yours! We know how researchers have their scientific achievements stolen by their bosses. It would be downright stupid to continue to grind here and let others take the credit! And by the way – money would no longer be a problem!'

No sooner said than done. Gustav scraped together his little bit of severance pay and founded the GustavLab GbR, Institute for Gene Therapy, together with a colleague who had also been fired – Klaus Femor – and with used equipment from his previous employer. He found suitable rooms in the local Technology and Start-Up Centre, where he was welcomed with open arms, because the building – an old barracks – had hardly been occupied for years. The initial core business of the new institute – against Melvil's advice – was genome sequencing for the police and other groups, which, however, did not get off to a good start due to the prevailing market oversaturation.

As his first official act, he made Moni the offer of a parttime job, which she could do alongside her studies and which she accepted to his great delight. Over the months, Monika had become a permanent fixture for Gustav, not only in the business, where she soon began to pull all the strings, but also at night, when Gustav stared at the blackness above his bed, where he thought he could see shadows of his beloved one. In erotic terms, however, not much came of it – he merely thought he recognised a certain gleam in her eyes when she bent down close to him at the desk to compare those ugly columns of figures.

Should he make another advance? She had put on a little weight, especially around her belly, but Gustav thought it looked good on her.

Maybe tomorrow would be the right time! Tomorrow – that would be his big day. His fifteen mice – yes, all fifteen were still alive – would break through the magical Methuselah barrier, which currently stood at a lifetime of six years, five months and twenty-eight days. How he had trembled that another researcher would come up with a new record during the last few months! He had meticulously searched through all scientific journals but had never found any evidence of such machinations. He would be the first! The article for the renowned magazine Nature Biotechnology was already completed and waiting on his desk at home.

With regard to this article, it is worth mentioning that Zehdenick did not give the exact recipe of the infusion solution, the nectarine. On the one hand, because he did not know it himself – although he had probably carried out over a hundred laboratory analyses – and on the other hand, because in the world of applied science it was generally not advisable to broadcast research results without protection. At the very least, they had to have been registered before with the national and international patent offices. And that was not possible because he could not give the details of his "invention". Melvil was no help to him there either. He knew everything about everything; but when it came to the elixir of life, he became taciturn and diverted to other topics. Well, maybe he would talk tomorrow. He had agreed to come. Somehow, it had to go on.

In fact, everything went smoothly the next day. Gustav did his normal work, only attracting the attention of his co-workers with his excessive nervousness and occasional clumsiness. Towards the end of the day, he sent Monika to get two bottles of Prosecco and some sandwiches, maybe a garland with a lantern. Confetti, if needed, could be taken from the hole punchers in abundance. (If necessary, the fragments from the shredders would also do.) He'd also had to integrate the trainee Peter into the team – with promises and threats –, whose curiosity had not missed the "eternal comparison group" with the black-spotted little animals. Where was Melvil? He arrived at half past five, the garland was already up, and music was playing softly from the small loudspeaker.

'If someone from the centre administration comes in and asks what we're doing here: Peter is celebrating his birthday. How old are you today?' said Gustav.

'Me? I haven't even…'

'How old!'

'Er… oh… twenty-five.'

But no one came, and so the small group, spearhead of occidental research in the field of molecular-biological gerontology, celebrated their success in merriment and exuberance in a quiet corner of the large Entrepreneur building, seemingly unnoticed. The two Prosecchi played their part too. Gustav even got carried away with a short speech, for which he took a mouse out of its cage, held it up and asked it to flex its upper arm and show its biceps – as a demonstration of its youthful vitality. The mouse was visibly vital (you could tell by the fact that it survived its master's violent gesticulation movements), but it didn't want to do such a stupid thing to itself. Melvil laughed and said Gustav had probably injected himself with a few ampoules of the nectarine solution, and that in any case, speaking of biceps, it was quite remarkable how easily he had lifted the mouse…

Eventually, in the course of the evening, the male interest turned more and more to the present lady, with Gustav being the active part, constantly snuggling up to her and bumping into her. She showed him the cold shoulder, while the other two confined themselves to gazing (Peter) and silent agreement (Melvil). The longer the evening went on, the more distracted the latter seemed. He lifted his nose again and again, and turned his head as if sniffing something approaching from far away.

'I think I must be off then,' he suddenly said, throwing his cloak over his shoulder in a perfect fold. 'I just remembered:

I have some business to attend to', he added, and was out of the room in a flash.

The noise that now began could not be classified as an earthly sound. A crash and a roar ran through the corridor, as if the sulphurous vents of Hades were opening here, on the second floor of the massive barracks building. The three researchers rushed out of the room. Melvil, who had grown to superhuman size, fought furiously with four peculiar figures – human- to dragon-like – who tugged him on all sides and tried to hold him down. White smoke, the stench of carob and faeces, sparks in all colours and repeated flashes of lightning rounded off the scene in a dramaturgically impressive way.

'Melly!' Holding her belly, Monika ran towards the fighters. They reached for her with incredibly long gibbon arms and soared, writhing and tangling. The ceiling didn't seem to be a barrier for them, they penetrated it effortlessly. Only Monika had problems. She struggled with all her might, her belly stuck a little in the woodwork, but then there was a jolt and she too was through. The whole spook was gone. Including Melvil and Monika.

Gustav and Peter stood motionless for a while, gawking. Then their jaws dropped again, and they shook their heads.

5.

Zeus lay languidly on his ottoman and cleared his throat. 'Can someone else do the negotiating?' he asks in a brittle voice. 'I'm so-so today.'

Jesus suggests his father, Yahweh, but almost all the other gods are against it. A god who considers himself the only one can hardly preside over a divine tribunal. The choice finally falls on old Tyr, who then also strides solemnly into the middle of the circle and looks around disapprovingly.

'The court lime tree is missing,' he observes.

Indeed, a proper Thing Site needs a lime tree. But such a thing is for gods, especially when it concerns the leading heads of the cosmos, even if one must note that many are absent today, be it because they do not feel well like Zeus, or because they sympathise with the delinquent – it is, of course, once again Prometheus… Such a thing is no problem for the gods, and – poof! a magnificent linden tree grows out of the Small Magellanic Cloud. When Loki has brought Tyr his prosthetic arm and taken a seat at his feet, everything is ready for the event.

Only the delinquent is still missing. He is dragged here by the Hellhound Garm and the Fenris Wolf, who has once again broken loose. Hades, by the way, would have had no problem lending out his hellhound Cerberus, since the accused has Greek roots, but Tyr (a cousin of Shiwa, by the way, and also a distant relative of Zeus) thought that if there was to be a Germanic Thing, then it should be at all Germanic. The fact that the accused was Greek did not bother him.

When Prometheus is finally lashed to the lime tree, kneeling and with his head bowed, flanked by the two salivating wolfish beasts, and the absence of the Goddess of Justice – unexcused as always – is noted, the trial can begin. In place of the goddess, Wen Chang, responsible for culture and literature and peripherally also for the legal system, reads out the indictment.

Who do you think could have drawn it up?

You think the Nordic Gods love the big scene, the constant battle, the approaching twilight or the end of the world – but deep down they are accountants, collectors, archivists. And they like to tinker with sophisticated projects (or how else can you explain the fjord coast of Norway?). This is also true of Bragi, who penned the elaborate work that is chiselled here in runes on a number of panels (vaguely reminding of tablet PCs). It is impossible to reproduce it verbatim at this point, because it is so long, complicated and convoluted.

In any case, the litany begins with the personal data of the accused: Prometheus, one of the Titans, son of Iapetus and Asia or Clymene or Gaia – the motherhood cannot be determined so precisely – creator and friend of mankind. Previously convicted of stealing the divine fire and bringing it to mankind, which in the long run led to freemasonry, enlightenment and this exuberant rationality, which is partly responsible for the decay of religion and thus for the current deplorable state of the divine world. Furthermore, he was suspected of having attempted or even caused similar things to happen on the planets of the systems Gliese and Kepler. The divine representatives of these heavenly bodies are to be heard on another day of the trial.

Furthermore: Serving a prison sentence of several hundred years by means of rock chaining in the area of the Caucasus in connection with regular corporal punishment by professionals or by liver eating on the part of the eagle Ethon. After this, a number of centuries insignificant or not known. With the new offence now on trial, he has apparently relapsed.

Yes, the current offence, as the statement of claim describes, is the "transfer of technological capabilities for the purpose of procuring eternal life to beings of inferior mental power conceived as mortals". In short, we have long suspected that this obscure Melvil in the Institute is actually Prometheus, and the equally mysterious "Nectarine" contains the formula for eternal human life. It can only be a matter of weeks until people have solved this mystery and will use the remedy on themselves en masse. Then, as is clear not only to the Olympians, these less gifted will have taken another step towards divinity, and it is only a matter of centuries until they will have climbed the logical further rungs, namely:

invulnerability
youthfulness
omniscience, omnipotence, etc., etc.

It should be noted that many gods also have their problems with these divinities. Was Kronos really so immortal when he was slain by his son Zeus? Or is he not dead at all, but is now doing his duty on Kepler 452 b, for example? But then something should have been heard from him! Whatever the case, quick intervention is called for if the further decay of faith, the progressive infideliosis or – brrr – "pale rot" of the world of the gods is to be stopped. Hence the "Special Unit Prometheus", which had suddenly appeared at the institute, arrested the target after a quick grab and transferred him to Cosmic Olympus. A certain Monika was also caught in the net, which turned out to be a stroke of luck, since this Earth woman was carrying or is still carrying the child of the target person in her womb. A future demi-divine, we shall see what happens to him. Hera, Zeus's wife, has fortunately experience in such matters.

While these iniuria are reported in all their details, Prometheus slumps more and more against the lime tree. He already knows what is coming. His fellow gods are not that imaginative. No, they will go back to the tried and tested. Not a nice thought. Even Garm and the Fenris wolf lie "flat down" on the ground and whimper softly.

6.

Through dark space flies the asteroid Hathor, a misshapen lump of rock, not unlike a large potato, with a chapped, jagged crust bearing countless scars from meteorite impacts. It orbits lonely around the earth's sun, which makes it boiling hot on the sunny side, while the dark side freezes in icy space. For its namesake, the beautiful ancient Egyptian goddess Hathor, responsible for love, this piece of debris was a pure imposition, the other gods thought. But Hathor had always refused to go against the naming. 'I, too, have my ugly side,' she said and quickly swallowed the sun god Re, whereupon – surprise, surprise – it did not get any darker in space. Undeterred by all this, the asteroid Hathor continues to orbit around the bright celestial star, occasionally coming dangerously close to planet Earth. 'If one day we should give up this tiresome experiment with humanity – and current events certainly suggest we should –' Loki had remarked at the recent Thing meeting, 'then this Hathor might well be an option.'

Although the humans usually put out feelers for everything that cavorts around their planet, inspecting it with telescopes, orbiters, lander robots, they have not been in a hurry with Hathor so far. So they hardly know how big the lump is in diameter (300 m?) or how long a "day" lasts on it. If they were to venture within a few hundred metres from it in a spaceship and point their instruments at the celestial body, they would hardly miss the figure that lies there stretched out lonely between rocky cliffs. Some would scratch their heads in amazement, for the man (recognisable by his beard) has no abdomen at all. I don't dare describe the gruesome scene in more detail, only this much: The man – or what is left of him – is moving. He is obviously still alive.

Shortly before the spaceship could initiate the landing approach to the rock splinter to provide first aid, it would undoubtedly be ordered back by Earth – because of the apparent discrepancy between the transmitted perceptions and the official reality.

We, however, are not bound by such conventions, we can see things as they are. We recognise that the man's blood flow is slowly coming to a halt, that his gaping wound is beginning to close, and indeed, as the site of the discovery slowly turns out of the sunlight, that his body seems to lengthen downward...

Night on Hathor.

... and that he has regained his full form by "sunrise". Incredible! We realise this person cannot be human, and when we notice the wrought-iron chains around his wrists that prevent him from standing up, we finally know: It can only be Prometheus, creator of man, bringer of fire and eternal life. The gods at the Thing had again no better idea than to forge him somewhere. And because it hadn't worked so well last time at the Caucasus, they had now taken this barren lump of stone, where not even a divine eagle would circle.

However, the lump is not quite so desolate after all. Although it is inhospitable, either too cold or too hot, and not endowed with any atmosphere, it is nevertheless the regular destination of divine flying visits. During the day, they are usually travelling groups of younger gods, demigods and auxiliaries who are to be shown the enforceability of the cosmic legal system. At other times, however, usually at dawn, when Prometheus has just regained his full form, he also receives private visitors.

Like now.

'Prome, Prome,' moans Athena, who has settled down on the barren rock in the shade of a parasol she has brought with her, and gently strokes his newly grown thigh. 'What have you done now? Did you have to do that? Haven't you had enough yet?'

Prometheus groans. The worry lines on his faithful friend's face do not bode well for him. Stuck for an eternity again? Under such disastrous circumstances? And no prospect of early release or liberation by a wandering hero? 'What is Heracles doing, by the way?' he asks wanly.

'Do you think he'll come and free you? Like last time?' Athena shakes her wise head. 'No, he'll not even think of it, don't get your hopes up. The gods are not well disposed towards you. It's not just our senile father of the gods. This time it's ALL of them!' She says it with such finality that all colour drains from Prometheus's face.

'But that little bit of nectarine I stole…'

'It's not about the nectarine. It's about the formula it contains! People have decoded it, as you know, and this Gustav, this researcher, has already published it in a scientific journal. He has even registered it as a patent! So now they have eternal life, the humans, just as you wanted. Congratulations! They now consider themselves gods.'

By now they are in the blazing sun. This asteroid also seems to rotate relatively fast, let's say at five-hour intervals. Athena rises, for which a little push with her hand is enough, because gravity is close to zero (it's more of a problem not to drift off into space), and repositions the umbrella. Then she reaches into her travel bag. 'Here, I brought you something,' she says, taking out souvlaki skewers wrapped in cloth, some toast and a jar of tzatziki. A bottle of Ambrosia Rosé peeps out of the bag.

Prometheus raises his head, squints at the delicious offerings, rattles his chains feebly, and lets himself sink back.

'Why bother?' he sighs. 'After all, everything is…' He keeps quiet about the rest.

'Eat!' says Athena firmly and holds out a skewer. 'You have to keep up your strength! After all, what you're going through here is not a recreational holiday. This is a punitive action. And who knows what else the gods will come up with in their wrath.'

Prometheus shakes his head, but then bites off a piece of meat and takes a sip of the wine. Suddenly – out of nowhere – an owl swoops in silently, circles the two of them and takes a seat on Athena's shoulder. She takes it gently in her hand (it is not very big, obviously a little owl) and puts it on her lap. 'Too much light is not good for a night bird,' she says. At the same time she cuddles the owl, which closes its big eyes with pleasure. The scene relaxes visibly and develops into a cosy one, in spite of all bad premonition.

'Now, let's get straight to the point,' Athena begins, after she has tidied up the leftovers. 'Why did you do that?'

'What?'

'Bring eternal life to the people.'

Prometheus grins. 'Wasn't that the logical next step?'

Athena assumes the thinking position (head on fist, elbow on knee) and looks at her friend scrutinisingly. 'That sounds like a plan.'

'Well spotted'.

'Would you tell me what it is?'

'I just like them, the humans. They've given us their faith for thousands of years. It's time to give them something back.'

'That sounds good, but it's not a plan.'

'Hmm… all right then, listen.'

'Athena, friend, you are the Goddess of Wisdom. As one can see from your owl. You are wise, and the others are stupid. Most of them, anyway. They are as clever as the inferior beings who believe in them. Partying, showing off, horsing around, bullying each other – that's how it goes every day. At the same time, they slaughter each other in the cruellest way. Or they are completely uptight, seclude themselves and dream fantasies of omnipotence. Like this Yahweh, for example. I don't understand how such a nerd can gather such a large fan community around him.'

The little owl's eyes widen. Athena nods, perhaps just to encourage him to keep talking.

'Yet he's doing alright! He's not as affected by infideliosis as our boss is, for example! No, Yahweh is still going strong! How does he do it? Though he obviously has ADD? Or is he autistic? He thinks he's supreme! Does he believe that this will make him popular in our circles? He wants everyone to give all their faith to him exclusively – sure, he wants all the energy for himself – and meanwhile spreads plagues, catastrophes, wars and whatnot. But that seems to be his recipe: spread misery so that hope becomes all the greater. And in the end, he sends them all to hell!'

'Jahweh is all right,' Athena interrupts him. 'There are worse.'

'That's what I mean!' Prometheus is now visibly agitated. 'They're all barmy. As long as this mongrel bunch is at the helm, nothing will get better in the universe!' He tries to straighten up but only produces a violent rattling of chains. (Which is astonishing, since no sound is transmitted in a vacuum. In this respect, all those blown-up science fiction films are also nonsense!)

Athena, as if to reflect on his words, carefully rises, whereby the owl – she calls him "Kiwitt" – jumps on Prometheus's leg, not without digging his claws into his flesh unintentionally. She reaches for the sunshade to adjust it once more to the position of the sun. Yes, this asteroid rotates quickly. When she has taken her seat and her bird again, he whispers weakly: 'My God, it will soon be night again.'

Athena nods. 'That's why you should finally get to the point.'

'We have to get rid of them!' he says in a firm voice. 'All that eerie vermin, get rid of it! The easiest way to do that is to give the inferior beings a little more intellect and thereby curb the power of belief on which we all live. That automatically leads to infideliosis, that is to say: to the decline and end of the divine pack.'

'That's an idiotic plan!'

'It's a brilliant plan!'

'Then you and I are also lost!' A wrinkle of annoyance stretches across her evenly chiselled forehead.

Prometheus grins.

It slowly dawns on Athena. 'Hey – you are not afflicted? But... where do you get the faith energy from? I've been wondering the whole time why you're so cheerful in spite of your current predicament. Who believes in you? Who even knows of your existence?'

'Wouldn't you like to know?'

'Well, it's striking.' Prometheus's suddenly brightened mood alienates her. One minute he was depressed, not to say tired of life. Now full of energy, like a workaholic.

'Have you actually noticed that there are some new members lurking around on the fringes of our meetings?' he asks, leaning on his elbows.

'I have. Strange characters. Kind of technical looking. Like knights. Or astronauts. Or that... that...'

'Darth Vader?'

'Exactly! From Star Wars!'

'That's not Darth Vader. That's Gugel'Huu. And then there are a few others. Mocelhand, Frazbuk, Ziwittziwitt, and Clontli, to name a few. And the old demon Mammon has now attained divine status as well!'

'And they are not affected by infideliosis?'

'No. These lords and ladies are doing splendidly. This is a whole new generation. Quite young. All hot. Thinking and feeling completely differently from the rest of us.' Prometheus goes into raptures. 'I'm telling you, they're the future. They're the gods that come after us. When our whole rotten club has died. You're not saying anything?'

'Nest fouler! Comrade pig! Traitor!' cries Athena. Her face has now assumed such a scowl that no archaeologist would have recognised her. 'That's disgusting! That's not like you! You think you're the supreme god here, the one who can decide who lives and who must die! No, I no longer understand why I came here. Come, Kiwitt, let's go!' The excited movements accidentally propel her five metres high, and she has to wave violently to reach the ground again. She still has to gather her things, after all.

'No, please, stay! You must hear the story to the end!' pleads Prometheus.

'I don't want to know anything so disgusting!' she exclaims, but after a minute's thought, she takes her seat again.

Those with ears to listen can hear their argument far out into space (see above for details). And they can also see it – after all, they are sitting on the sunny side of the asteroid Hathor. On the dark side, however, it is as gloomy as night or like the rest of space, which is starry but cold and hostile to life. If one were to sit in the aforementioned spaceship and take a closer look at the dark side, one could easily discover numerous shimmering spots of light, like the scales of a reptile, which now and then seem to be stirred up in rapid movement, only to calm down again for a while. Equipped with a powerful night-vision device, we would know what or who we were looking at: it is Apophis, the giant serpent from ancient Egyptian times, a thoroughly evil deity, optimally made for the task that followed from the Thing's draconic verdict.

But its hour has not yet come. One wonders, of course: Can Apophis hear what Prometheus is babbling about? And pass it on to his fellow gods? After all, he too would be a potential victim of Prometheus's wicked plan!

But no, everyone knows that snakes can't hear anything. They have no ears.

'Is there a religion somewhere for these weird birds?' inquires Athena. 'Are they visiting us? From some parallel universe?'

'It doesn't need religion. It only needs faith, the energy of faith. And, believe me, the new ones truly have enough of that. Enough that they can still share it with us. This is our chance, we have to keep at it, otherwise we'll go down like the others. It's like this: Gugel'Huu and Co, these weird birds, as you call them, embody the new divine civilisation. Binarism. They are digital deities, so to speak. Virtual-transcendent. People believe in them without realising it. That's the joke! Just like they believe in technological progress, for example!'

'Don't know that one. Is that a god too?'

'A very old one. From ancient times. "Wheel" is his name. You really don't know him?'

'Never seen him before.'

'No wonder. Wheel keeps himself to himself, doesn't want to have anything to do with us. Just like the new guys he cooperates with. We're too conservative for him.'

Athena gently scratches the back of her owl's neck, lost in thought. Then she shakes her head. 'So it's a plot!' she sums up. 'You're planning a coup!'

'There would be a place for a goddess of spirit and wisdom too, I think.'

'Haha, good one. And what is to come out of the coup?'

'The whole divine ragtag will be deposed, and we will take its place.'

'My goodness! The same old story again.'

'Yes, the usual. Us, the good guys, against them, the bad old guys. If we don't do it, others will.'

'Then let them do it!'

'It's better if one of us – or both of us – have the finger in it, so it won't go wrong. I'm still not clear: Can the newcomers be trusted? When you ask them what they want, they just say they don't really know. The future is so full of possibilities that nothing can be said. No one had foreseen the unbelievable spread of mobile phones. And then there's the fact that the newcomers don't have any experience yet. I just say: androids.'

Athena looks at him, lost in thought again. Can she believe all this? Aren't these just fantasies, delusions of one eternally doomed? Who wouldn't try to escape such an inescapable fate if only it were possible? But what if he spoke the truth? Then it would be an attempted coup d'état, a conspiracy between Prometheus and the strange, inhuman god-beings whose plans no one knows. Yes, it is about the abolition of the old gods, and the new ones taking their place. A vicious plan!

'Prome, let's be honest. Could it be that you just want revenge? For what they did to you? For your suffering at the Taurus? And for all this here…?' She does not voice what is inevitably to come.

Prometheus shrugs his shoulders, as if he doesn't understand what she is saying, and directs his gaze thoughtfully at his scantily covered, still healed abdomen. With half-closed eyes, he smiles silently and murmurs barely audibly: 'Athena, you know me! I'm always trying to be factual! And if it looks like revenge – what can I do?'

The sun is now low over the horizon. Such a day on Hathor is over quickly, it barely lasts a prison visit. Kiwitt on Athena's shoulder is already turning his head restlessly in all directions and looking expectantly at his mistress. She stands up cautiously, peers suspiciously at the horizon, goes to the umbrella, which is now already a few metres away, and folds it up.

'Night will come soon,' Prometheus sighs. His voice sounds as limp again as it did at the beginning. Is it the low sun that makes his face look so pale? 'Untie me, Athena, I know you can!' he pleads, trembling.

Athena places the umbrella in a gap between the rocks.

'I'll leave it here. No one will steal it,' she states and sits down again. 'Yes, it will soon be dark. And: no, I can't untie you. The gods are more furious than myth has ever known. Even if they don't know your plan, one thing is clear to them: You are the cause of their suffering. In the end, we would both languish here in fear.' She gathers up the dinner service, wraps it in a large linen cloth and puts it in her travelling bag. 'But say again, what did you mean about the androids just now?'

'Untie me first!'

'No!' She doesn't say it, but her expression betrays what she is thinking.

'Oh, come on!'

'So – the androids…'

'All right then – the androids. We know that humans are in the process of building technological beings that are like them. And can also multiply and even evolve themselves!'

'Yes, thanks to your beneficial work, they can! Lem told us about it at the Thing. But what's the problem?'

'Will androids believe in anything?'

'Oh… now I see. But as long as there are humans or other lower beings, it doesn't matter!'

'Yes, as long as! That's where the problem lies. You remember: This little paltry god Lem was of the opinion that the androids might find the softies or jelliers, as Lem also calls them, annoying in the long run. I'd hate to be more specific than that, you know?'

'Hmm. I know you can see the future.'

Prometheus sighs. 'Let's look ahead instead,' he says.

'Which brings us back to the beginning,' Athena says, starting to walk away. 'What's the point of all this? What do you get out of it?'

'The cosmos has to become more reasonable. That's all there is to it. That's all I want. That's how I've always been. And you too. And some others, Hathor for example. We are the gods of spirit and reason. It's beastly, isn't it, the way things are going at present?'

Athena stands still for a moment, her travelling bag already in her hand, as if considering his words, then leans towards him and bids him farewell with pecks on both cheeks.

'Untie me,' he whispers one last time. In vain.

In the last ray of the sun, Athena rises up in the "air" with her bag, accompanied by the little owl, waves down once more and calls out, 'See you tomorrow!' Then she sets course for cosmic Olympus. Soon the asteroid Hathor shows itself to her as the big potato we know it to be. The sky is clear, the visibility good – it will be a smooth flight. In the distance, amidst the other coloured spirals and mists, she can already see the small Magellanic Cloud, where the Thing meeting had taken place. But she doesn't want to go there; her goal is Cosmic Olympus, the dwelling place of the great Olympians, of whom she is one.

Suddenly the little owl, who is taking the journey on Athena's shoulder, cries out 'kiwitt, kiwitt!' in the highest excitement. Anyone who knows anything about owls knows that the cry of a little owl can never mean anything good. And anyone who sees what the animal has spied will be horrified and no longer happy.

In the darkness of Hathor's night side, Apophis has awakened. His thousands of colourful scales shine between the rocks where he had been hiding, and move in seemingly directionless serpentine lines towards the twilight zone. His tongue, probably as long as a chariot (with horses!), flickers sharply through the rock, his eyes glowing with hatred, his hissing and the noise of his rattles at the end of his tail sounding loud. As if by chance, but inexorably, he approaches the place where Prome lies forged to the rock. Athena sees him writhing with all his might in the chains, as Aphobis straightens up in front of him, his evil gaze fixed on his victim, and then with lightning speed and vehemence...

We know the rest.

Athena's and Prometheus's screams resound far and wide through space and shake the gods to the core, especially those who are all-knowing and thereby of course also all-hearing. Even these inhumanes, accustomed to bestiality and blood-baths, shudder at the notion of the event, which they have fortunately to witness only very indirectly.

Athena has also turned her face away at first. But in a moment she has to look again: Prometheus's blood is flowing in streams from his belly, his hips with the legs bitten off are hanging crosswise in the snake's mouth. He is shaking them back and forth to get them into a position where he can devour them. Those readers who exuberantly sympathise with Prometheus may be reassured: Prometheus no longer feels pain, he is unconscious. The snake Apophis looks around with satisfaction. He is full, he has done his job properly today, and what is perhaps even more important: He has once again polished up his image as a profoundly evil deity. And tomorrow it will be the same game again: He will be well provided with work and food for the next thirty thousand years. Maybe even longer.

If only it weren't for this strange tiredness!

7.

In a spacious villa, almost a castle, Gustav Zehdenick sits in a large living room, more like a hall, and plays chess with his favourite android. Everything in this room is noble, reminiscent of a baronial mid-nineteenth century salon. But we are far from that era, and although we met Gustav in the thirties of the twenty-first century (he was almost in his prime then), we have now passed three hundred years, and Gustav is still there. Yes, he is there, seemingly alive and well.

However, on closer inspection, one may notice some oddities about him: the head appears youthful, but the neck is full of wrinkles. One arm is normal, though full of liver spots, the other pale with translucent veins. His manner of speaking is also abnormal – his speech sounds monotonous, sometimes halting, and with a faltering voice at the end of each sentence. The android seems, in comparison, more alive.

The android is making a move with his bishop and says in a melodious voice: 'Check!' Gustav, somewhat confused, sighs audibly, and without thinking moves his king another step towards the corner. If you wanted to look inside the android – his name is Andi, by the way – to see what is going on in this creature made of titanium, carbon and glass fibres, you would notice some components running hot and chips fluttering. For the courtesy module implanted in it (as in all newer items of this series) forbids it to beat its master for the third time today. Andi is allowed to win 62.75 per cent of all games in a month, otherwise he is automatically put into safe mode. No wonder the beads of sweat are forming on his brow.

Speaking of brows – you have to imagine him very human-like in shape, but the materials have been left undisguised so that you can recognise him as an artificial being. The members of the social upper class – and there is almost only this upper class left, the lower class has been "worn out" or gently disposed of – attach great importance to this difference.

Yes, Andi, what's left for you? Try a draw, if he moves further into the corner, the chances are good. A draw is not counted. It's not a victory for your master, but it does have a certain sporting touch for him.

While they are lost in thought, staring at the board with the few remaining pieces, the news programme of the day is playing on the video wall with the sound turned off. Once again, everything is atrocious, both in terms of domestic and foreign politics, if one still wants to classify the war with WESPAC, which has been going on for over two hundred years, as "politics". The lack of sound makes everything even more sinister. In addition, the colour sometimes fails or only flashes briefly, or falls from one monochrome display to another.

But the "Latest from the Neighbourhood" is no more edifying: the recent genetic experiments that have led to people with three heads, new diseases with pandemic potential, bizarre crimes and the situation with the current uprisings in the country. Did I say the lower class has been wiped out? Yes, because the upper classes considered them superfluous and loved to use them up in the ongoing wars.

But there is still the middle class. It is rather small, but present everywhere and indispensable. Like Gustav Zehdenick's family doctor, who regularly gives him his nectarine cocktail. Or the team of technicians who maintain the house technology. Although a lot is already done by androids. Yes, they are more resilient and willing. And above all, more reliable.

Now the technician Donald enters the room. Donald comes because Andi has called him to look after the broken television.

'Not now!' Gustav yells at him and has the threatened king in his hands again. To the left! Andi thinks, and sure enough, Gustav moves it to the left. 'Draw!' Andi shouts sorrowfully and wipes the sweat from his brow. And inwardly breathes a sigh of relief. (None of this is true, but we know what is meant.)

The technician looks at the chaotic TV picture. It shows insurgents burnt to death by EMP cannons. He shakes his head. 'This can't be fixed. It all has to be replaced.'

Andi gazes absent-mindedly at the screen. This sentence is also found in his software, his master could have got that cheaper.

'How long will it take?' asks Gustav.

'A fortnight for sure!' says Donald.

Gustav is about to flare up. Two weeks! Two weeks in which he will have to deal with the various smaller screens scattered throughout the house. 'Will the other displays work?' he asks cautiously.

'Well, for one or two days, the whole system must be shut down. But we'll do the complete annual maintenance right away, so this way you'll save some time.'

What the board game had failed to do, this wretch of a technician has now accomplished: Gustav is checkmate. That to him! Isn't he one of the most respected dignitaries in town? If not the most respected? After all, he brought eternal life to the people, back then, three hundred years ago. Well, not to all people, but to his high society pals, to whom he was henceforth allowed to belong. And now he has to live under such paltry system failures? Watch his favourite soap opera on a small TV set? Probably with a magnifying glass in his hand? Unbelievable! Gustav suppresses a curse.

'All right, if it has to be,' he grumbles. 'When do you start?'

The technician pushes his lower lip forward thoughtfully. 'In three weeks?'

'Whaaaat?' Gustav wants to jump up, but various niggles and aches make him sink back into the chair. Instead, he pours out a bucket of curses on the poor professional, all in that monotone speech of a sick man who can hardly breathe. Andi kicks him in the shins under the table.

'Well,' Donald says, shrugging his shoulders. 'The staff shortage, you know. If the management thinks they have to replace the whole staff with androids – fine! And if those then break down in droves…'

'What? I thought they were less prone to failure than humans?'

'Haha, who told you that? The commercials? On the big screen? You know, that might have been the case in the past, with the robots that still ran on steam, so to speak…' What follows is a technical lecture on the development of androidism, which Gustav can only break off with difficulty.

Gustav sits there and remains silent. The technician has left the room. The big TV picture is switched off. Andi tilts his head and says, 'Okay, I'll go and do my update now. Is that all right?'

Gustav nods, and Andi rolls out of the room on his wheeled telescopic stilts. His master remains seated, deep in thought, at the table with the chessboard, next to which the beaten pieces lie.

What a load of shit is all this! He hadn't been feeling well already in the morning. This nectarine therapy is a delusion, not at all refined, like all this technical stuff. It works differently on all the organs, some age, others don't, others seem to rejuvenate every day. What a feeling! It's as if you're made up of mismatched spare parts. If he hadn't already invested so much money in this treatment... he drops the idea. He doesn't want to kill himself, that's for sure. Perhaps one day the technical progress... by the way: where is Melvil?

Three hundred years ago, when he brought him the potion, he had promised to come by regularly and provide some support if needed. And how often has he kept his promise since then? I'll tell you: not once! Another charlatan! You really can't trust anyone, not even a genius like this drinks-stall-owner Melvil! Weren't they about to launch the next coup: rejuvenation? With the means at hand, you can prolong your life, if you don't die violently, forever. Even in old age. But you remain what you are: a doddering old man or woman. With a prick or breasts down to the knees. If, on the other hand, it is possible – and it is obviously possible, as Melvil said – to rejuvenate the body, then that is the next logical step. He would like to meet anyone who would not make use of it! Including himself.

Gustav remembers that he is thirsty. The two glasses on the table are empty (the android's glass was cleaning fluid). He calls Andi and orders another glass of cognac.

That tin idiot could have noticed for himself that my glass was empty, he thinks. When will these machines finally grow up? He rises, grabs his glass and drags himself into the adjoining room. It is his study. It is as large and empty as the living room. In a corner against the wall is his desk with the network technology. A monitor is also on this wall, but much smaller than the other one.

Gustav switches it on to continue watching the war reports. The EURA units have just achieved remarkable successes in recapturing Greenland. There are crashes and flashes on the screen, Gustav really comes alive. It's a shame the picture is so small. Soon we'll have the whole Polar Sea, he thinks with satisfaction. And with it all the raw materials there.

It's just a pity that the war (it's called a "hot war") has caused the ice sheet of the mini-continent to melt alarmingly and the sea level to rise accordingly. That doesn't exactly make it easier to dig up the treasures! This should have been taken into account when programming the war automatons! He is sure of that.

Because this war of the EURA against the WESPAC is fully automated. The people actively involved can be counted on one hand. The passive participants – the victims of the civilian population – number in the thousands. But fortunately, there are fewer and fewer of them. Both victims and civilians at large. People who can afford to live forever are not among them. Those who have invested so much money in their therapy will surely not wantonly expose them to the risk of war! That would be a classic bad investment.

Now you see a squad of androids marching through a wall of fire. They walk through it as if nothing is wrong. A grenade explodes nearby, some of them fall down. The others don't care and walk on, unmoved. That's the beauty of these tin soldiers! You don't have to worry about casualties. Suicide squads are not an issue either. Gustav finds that this brings a completely different dynamic to the events.

And these fully autonomous droids. They can repair themselves. Yes, even manufacture themselves, imagine that! He saw a report the other day (this man apparently only sits in front of the television) about an android factory where only droids work. Droids create androids! They should also be used much more in the civilian sector. That technician from before! That was a joke! A droid could have done that in half an hour! And he wouldn't even ask for a tip!

And that idiot Andi would have noticed by himself that my glass was empty!

8.

Zeus is lying in bed. It's the middle of the day. On the left edge of the bed sits his wife Hera, on the right his daughter Athena. Their mood is gloomy. At the foot of the bed stands Asclepius, rummaging through his medical kit. He takes out a pendulum and asks Athena to step aside so that he can take her place. Then he bends over Zeus and lets the pendulum swing over his forehead.

'Cut the crap,' Zeus says quietly. His face is white as cheese; cramps shake him from time to time. 'Your remedies haven't helped so far, so all this bamboozling won't help either.'

'But it's about the flow of energy!' insists Asclepius. 'With the help of the pendulum, we can redirect and concentrate the free faith energy that is everywhere in the room…' He doesn't get any further, because Zeus grabs the pendulum and makes it disappear under the bedspread.

'Please!' says the doctor and holds out his open hand to him.

On the little commode on the wall is an amphora labelled Nectarine Essence with the note 'Do not use undiluted! Keep out of the reach of children! Empty amphora must be disposed of in an environmentally friendly way' and other well-intentioned instructions. The vessel is empty, Zeus has drunk the contents, we suspect, completely undiluted. But obviously, it has only helped a little.

Asclepius stows away his pendulum with a gruff expression, while Athena resumes her seat and places her hand on Zeus's forehead, which is cold rather than hot. Zeus closes his eyes, and for a moment it seems as if he wants to gently fall asleep. But suddenly he jerks up a little, a smile on his face. 'That reminds me,' he says, 'I wanted to tell you a joke!'

'Of course.' Hera is visibly pleased by her husband's sudden verve. 'Tell!'

'Well, it goes like this: Mercurius – no, Hermes – well, never mind… where was I?'

'The joke! You were going to tell it.'

'Oh, right. So Hermes flies the captive balloon over the rocks from Kepler number… I don't remember the number, it doesn't matter. He got lost in space and now he's asking the alien below… wait, I'm getting it… asking him… oh, asking him where he is. Er… '

My God, thinks Hera, this could take a while. But we all know the punch line. 'And then the alien says…', she helps him.

'Yes, the alien says… you are Hermes! Yes, that's right!'

Hera shakes her head in distress. How confused he is today. Now he's told the joke a hundred times and can't get it together. 'You must be a computer scientist,' she corrects him.

'What? Oh yes… you must be Hermes!'

It's no use. He's never been this lame before. She gives Athena a sorrowful look, who responds in the same way. Both goddesses worry not only about their husband, brother and father, but also about him as the father of the gods, about the whole family of gods, about the greater whole. Apropos, the greater whole – what is left of it? Things have not turned out for the best in the last three hundred years.

No, things have rather turned out as Thot had prophesied at the memorable Thing meeting – infideliosis has taken hold insidiously, killing one immortal after the other. It's made and still makes (almost) no difference between the religions, perhaps more so between the planets. Only half of the earthly gods are still alive, and it has to be said that even Hera – unlike Athena – does not look particularly spry.

Last but not least, Quetzalcoatl, the feathered serpent, had lost her iridescent plumage (at first she had claimed this was just the way of the moult and that it was quite normal), and now she lies curled up in the corner, grey and shaggy.

Only the new gods, and with them a few old ones, including Athena, seem unaffected by the plague. (We can't see it now, but we can guess: Prometheus is also doing well under these circumstances). No, they have thrived in the last centuries. So there is really no need to fear that heaven will be completely empty in the future.

While Asclepius and the two women are consulting a few steps away from the foot of the bed about what else can be done, it happens: A clattering sound is heard from the bed, it is the bedpan Zeus had thrown out when he writhed with cramps. Startled, everyone rushes over, even the Coatl has his eyes wide open. Zeus has sunken back into the pillows, his eyes twisted, his mouth open. Oh no, oh no! He too now! Hera and Athena and all the remaining all-knowing gods are beside themselves, as far as their weak condition allows them. Father of us all! It is a tragedy! What is to be done now? Who will take Zeus's place? This Coatl? As if he'd read their thoughts (which he had actually done), he shakes his head wearily. Or Vishnu or Shiva? Speaking of Shiva, does he actually still dance? Yes, he does, if you want to interpret sitting down with flicking thumbs as dancing.

The news of Zeus's death spreads quickly in cosmic Olympus and far beyond. His not unexpected but sudden demise raises questions upon questions: When will the funeral be? Will it be confined to the small circle of the remaining Olympians – i.e., Hera, Athena, Poseidon and Artemis? That would be best for most of them, because hardly anyone is still fit enough for the stresses and strains that such an event entails.

And then: Who will succeed Zeus? Hera? Athena? Poseidon? Or an alien god? It is clear that the cosmic background noise has increased immensely since Zeus's death. What most old gods don't think about: Gugel'Huu doesn't doubt for a moment that this role will fall to him. Gugel'Huu, who looks like a giant plasticine figure, blacker than the night, overflowing with endlessly upward or downward flickering luminous lines, accompanied by his no less bizarre henchmen Frazbuk, Ziwittziwitt and the like. Now, he thinks, now is the moment. But – don't rush things! Just don't overheat the processors now! Stay cool! Everything will sort itself out.

9.

The gods with earthly roots have gathered again on the Thing Square of the Small Magellanic Cloud. They want to elect a new father or mother of the gods. Gugel'Huu and his entourage have taken up residence at the edge of the site. They know they are not particularly popular with the old dignitaries, and prefer to keep a low profile. Until their time comes. Athena and Wheel are also sitting with them.

We will spare ourselves the description of the nomination and the discussions – we know democracy, the procedure is not very pleasant and usually drags on endlessly with numerous repetitions. Again and again, the speakers deviate from the topic and deal with the predicament of divinity, reverently paraphrasing the essential issues, but beyond recognition.

Thus, the proceedings ripple along until Thot suddenly asks the question about a higher being.

How? The higher beings are US!

'No, I mean an even higher being. A supreme god, so to speak.'

The participants of the meeting are confused. What is this now? What does this have to do with the election?

'I just mean a supreme being could save us!'

I see. Hmmm… it's not such a far-fetched thought. It takes a while to take root in the minds of the gods. Some already look confident, others consider it a bitter irony. You can see exactly where the line runs between atheists and believers.

'But that's complete nonsense,' exclaims Mammon, who is not sitting with the dissidents but in the midst of the old-timers. 'There are no higher beings! (than us, he forgets to say). It's all just talk, there's not a shred of proof!'

The others shake their heads. Everyone knows there can be no proof. Or, strictly speaking: there MUST not be! Because if there were, there would be no need to believe. And where there is no faith, there is no energy of faith. The result: Infideliosis!

'I mean,' Mammon corrects himself, 'there is no evidence. If there were a higher being, it would have made itself known somehow. And more than that: It would never have let it come to this. What kind of God is that? Who on the one hand is supposed to protect us and on the other lets us die in the process!'

'God's ways are mysterious,' says Wen Chang.

Author's note: In order to distinguish between the gods and the presumed *super god*, we will call the latter from now on "Su'Go". And to avoid entanglements in the hawsers of correctness, we declare that if he/she existed, he/she would be genderless or a neuter: Su'Go is an "IT"! Now let's continue with the story...

'Let's try a thought experiment... ', says Thot, and steps into the circle. (Oh God, this is the head of a consulting firm speaking! Now we're supposed to come up on our own with the ideas he's wanting to foist on us!) He can't stand Wen Chang, who is always trying to steal contracts from him. 'If we haven't believed in Su'Go so far, then it never existed. Unless the gods of other planets believed in "IT". Everyone knows that we gods exist only on the basis of the faith of mortals, or so-called mortals. Where there is no faith, there is no God. It's as simple as that.'

Enamoured by his conclusive presentation, he looks around triumphantly, but no one applauds. 'Then the reverse is true: If we believe in Su'Go, then it exists!' he continues. 'That means we can save ourselves by starting to believe in our Saviour.'

Ah! Aha! That seems logical! Now a jolt goes through the plenum. As apathetically and absentmindedly as the gods sat there before, they now attentively follow every word.

'Well, it goes something like this,' says Thot and puts on an important expression that looks rather grotesque on his bird's head. 'We'll try a simple version first. Repeat after me!' Thot spreads his arms, pauses for a moment and then solemnly declaims, 'Oh Su'Go! Thou art the greatest god among all! Save us! Save us!' At this, he bows and crosses his arms in front of his forehead (as far as an ibis can be said to have a forehead). 'Now everybody! Big Su'Go! You greatest...' He looks around. No one follows his lead. 'You can do better! I know you can!' he shouts to the crowd. He pulls together all the knowledge he has from water gymnastics, where he regularly joins other gods to stay at least reasonably fit.

'Stand up straight for now. Otherwise, you won't be able to bow. Am I right?'

Grumbling, the gods stand up. Now he has them. No slacking now. 'We'll start small. ‚Oh Su'Go!' Repeat after me!'

'Oh Su'Go!' the gods cry.

'Fine! You can do it! Now again, with a bow!'

And so on and so forth. After a quarter of an hour, everyone is in tune and so intoxicated that some are already beginning to really believe in the existence of Su'Go. The whole cosmos seems to alternate in all colours. ... If I were Su'Go, I would start existing now.

Then Gugel'Huu joins the discussion. The dissident group has so far sat unmoved, listening with interest to Thot's words, but not participating in the new rite. 'Brothers! Sisters! I thank you. Thanks to all!' announced Gugel'Huu in a solemn tone. 'Please! Thank you! Be quiet for a moment! Please! Thank you!' Indeed, the first ones come to themselves; slowly, the LaOla of piety ebbs away.

'Thank you for your prayers! It has done me good! It has given me strength! The strength of faith that we all lack so much!'

The gods rub their eyes. Is this our Su'Go, they ask themselves. Has It been dwelling among us all this time? Then the whole system Thot has explained to us is void... Only very few think the latter.

Thot, being something of a smart cookie, sensed a new field of business. 'Oh Su'Go!' he cries, throwing himself lengthwise on the ground in front of Gugel'Huu. 'Highest God! Unmoved mover! Ens a nobis! Supreme truth! Word of the word! Breeder of the egg!' Even now, one has to acknowledge without envy, he's got it. Gugel'Huu raises his hands placatingly, but Thot will not be restrained. 'All-gracious! Bringer of salvation! Our saviour! Redeemer! Give us back our strength! Deliver us from the foul infideliosis! We believe in you! (Completely nonsensical, see above.) Yes, we believe...' That's as far as he gets, Gugel'Huu has stepped on his beak.

'Make haste, my children,' Gugel'Huu says solemnly. It's working, he thinks to himself. My goodness, how stupid can one be! It works! He would have liked to jump in circles. But his new function demands everything but that of him. So he looks down in a fatherly manner on his newly engaged high priest and says: 'Stand up, my son. Your faith has helped me. Yes, you have spoken the truth: The cosmos needs a completely new energy management concept. Sustainability is the order of the day! (He still has to practise the divine duct!) I have come to implement it. Soon you will be rid of your worries.'

At this, his eyes flash wickedly.

10.

The supergod Su'Go sits in his super cosmos and looks down at the many parallel universes at his feet. It would not be immediately recognisable to our eyes as a celestial being, for its shape resembles that of a large amoeba, and strictly speaking, they are not its feet but false feet, as we know from our biology lessons. Of course, Su'Go is not a single-celled organism, that should be noted in passing. Such categories do not exist in the super cosmos. But its shape is perhaps an indication of the possible circularity of all being, that is, the largest is equal to the smallest. Or something like that.

Su'Go's facial expression is troubled, almost worried, because IT does not like what is happening in space. It's not that the passing of the mishmash of gods makes IT sick to ITs stomach - that's peanuts in cosmic dimensions - no, IT is interested in certain aspects of these events. It is about a fundamental problem! It is about a question that comes up again and again, the solution to which IT still hasn't found, after aeons of relevant brooding. The question is: Am I actually the only sensible one here? Truly, the question is not that stupid.

Once, let's say three billion years ago, Su'Go was not yet so depressed. Back then, everything still seemed hopeful, everything was still in flux. Things were not yet so encrusted, trapped in eternal routines. Back then, IT was still full of confidence that one day it would be possible to form a beautiful heavenly garden out of the whole tangle of matter lumps and mists. A garden of Eden! For ITS own pleasure and that of the living creatures that filled it. But alas! What has become of it?

Three billion years of evolution – and that means hard creative work, just look at the complexity of a single living cell! – and all for nothing! Everywhere you look – and Su'Go can look everywhere at the same time – chaos, war, decay, disease, suffering, and death.

What went wrong? IT scratches ITS head (as far as one can speak of "scratching" in the case of amoeba pseudopods). IT has been asking ITself this question for about twenty-five million years (give or take twenty million, depending on the habitability of the celestial bodies) and still hasn't found a satisfactory answer. At least IT has a hypothesis: the introduction of intelligence played a part.

'May I say something?' (Who is speaking?)

'I don't like you talking about "IT" when you mean me. I'm not an animal!'

(Hey – Su'Go?)

'Is there anyone else here? So – please, no more "IT" when you're talking about me!'

(Honestly? Youuu? What a surprise!)

'Don't pretend. As if you've never dealt with me before. Alright?'

(What *alright*? Oh, the "IT". Yeah, maybe we could make something out of "he" and "she". "HESHE", perhaps? Or "SHEHE"?)

Isn't that a little childish? But it sounds better than… "IT".'

(Got it. "HEN"!)

'Who came first, the hen or the egg? How did you come up with "HEN"?'

(The Swedes invented the word. It is a gender-neutral pronoun. We could adopt it into English, then we'd be a bit global).

Su'Go shakes his head, if one can speak of a head in the case of a clod-shaped structure. 'Well, then I like "HESHE" best.'

(Even if the "he" really stands out at the front?)

'Or rather the "SHEHE"?'

(Yes, I think that's best. I think the masculine appeal is neutralised by having "she" at the beginning).

'All right, then.'

(And now?)

'What *now*?'

(Where were we? Oh yes, at the introduction of reason. But wait a minute, I'll go up to your level first – it's easier to talk there. So – let's put the brackets away!'

'Introduction of intelligence. Not reason. Unfortunately.' Su'Go leans back and crosses two pseudo pods over his pseudo stomach. 'Because the thing is, introducing intelligence into living beings is actually a cakewalk. We don't want to discuss this in detail here, otherwise, we'll get from the hundredth to the thousandth. In any case, the fact is that in practise it always goes wrong: The creatures harm themselves or beat each other to death.'

'Then you have to strengthen the instinctual equipment. Killing is not on! It's forbidden!'

'Wise guy! Intelligence is not possible with such rules. It includes freedom of mind!'

'Well, then I don't know…'

'And when the intelligent creatures realise that not only the grandmas and grandpas will die, but that one day it will be their turn, it will be all over. Then chaos will break out. We have come up with an artifice: The belief in supreme beings. It provides the right morals. Morality stabilises a bit...'

'But when I look at people's morals...'

'Right. Doesn't work either. They've created gods that look like themselves: They gorge and whore, beat their mothers and fathers to death ... I don't even want to think about that. And they have no character. Until now, they thought they were the greatest, now they worship me and beg for help. And then this scoundrel, Gugel'Huu. Impersonates me! Let himself be worshipped as Su'Go! I'll give him a run for his money!' Su'Go snorts in annoyance. 'So, these kinds of gods have nothing to do with me.'

'I thought so. You, on the other hand, seem quite nice.'

A glow of colour passes through the author's room.

'Thank you, I can return the compliment. Back to the subject at hand, we're going to try a new strategy.'

'And that would be?'

'Immortality. We're trying that out on Earth right now. We're going to start by giving people a much longer life. Two hundred to three hundred years. Have you heard of that?'

'Yes, I read about it once in a novel. Prometheus and all that.'

'We – my team and I – hope to stabilise the behavioural framework through life experience. Which will then be passed on to the younger generations. Because one thing is clear: Anyone who has invested so much money in prolonging his life will not risk it lightly!'

'True again.' The author pauses to write. 'I'm off for a moment.' He gets up and goes to the kitchen to make himself a cappuccino. In his mind, he is counting up the stock of his financial investments. He wouldn't even have enough for a drop of nectarine, that much he realises. But nothing has happened yet, it's all still in his head.

Speaking of which – off for a moment is good. Su'Go is everywhere, even in the kitchen. Here SHEHE continues with HERHIS remarks:

'At the same time, we are doing away with the old gods. They were a failure, you have to come to terms with that.'

'I think so too. I also left the church…'

'You wanted to save collection money, confess!'

'That's a malicious…'

'Okay, okay, forget it. And in the second step, we aim for rejuvenation.'

'And if that goes wrong again?'

They are now back in the author's study. The cappu with a white bonnet stands fragrantly before the monitor.

Su'Go sighs deeply. Indeed, nothing in life is certain. 'We still have some experiments running on other planets. Zeus's father Kronos on Kepler No. 452 b, do you remember?'

'Vaguely. And if that doesn't work either…?'

'Then I'll send the androids,' Su'Go groans. The thought seems to trouble HERHIM. But then SHEHE looks firmly down at the author again. 'You know, it's not the same. Androids don't believe in anything. They reproduce like water fleas. By the way, there you can see the difference between intelligence and wisdom. Androids are intelligent, but not wise. Like felons.'

'What does wisdom involve, if you don't mind me asking?'

'You may. Well, I would say embedded intelligence. The consideration of feeling, including empathy. The recognition of a deeper sense.'

'A deeper sense?'

'A sense of individual life. One may choose it oneself. To support this, we have created some people who have thought and taught in this direction. Confucius. Buddha. Or the philosopher Russell, for example.'

'I always seem to pick nonsense.'

'Nonsense! By the way, I once read a beautiful saying,' Su'Go says changing the subject, as if SHEHE has been surprised by HERHIS own memory. 'It goes,

> "The good life is one inspired by love and guided by knowledge".'

'You wouldn't believe I know it. From Bertrand Russell, isn't it?'

'You're a very literate reader.'

'Thank you. And you are a particularly benevolent god, if I may say so as an atheist.'

'I see we understand each other.'

The cappuccino still looks delicious and is waiting for its first sip. That's the beauty of it: It stays warm for a long time. Probably because of the milk cap, which insulates. And if you add pharisee-like a glass of rum, no one smells a thing.

Epilogue

Zeus died in our story, although he belonged to the "immortals", and was even one of their highest representatives. But immortality has always been mysterious, as we have seen with Zeus's father, Kronos, who was slain by his son.

This characterises the situation today quite well.

The immortality of human beings is only a question of time, it is said. The instruments, by which is primarily meant genetic engineering, seem to be already available, but it is still not yet known exactly what causes us to deteriorate and finally die after a certain age. As, incidentally, all more highly developed living beings do.

In 1990, Wikipedia listed about 300 theories about ageing. But none has yet brought a breakthrough. The guru of eternal life, AUBREY DE GREY, a British biogerontologist, says it will take about a quarter of a century. Then the first human being (Aubrey?) will be launched into immortality.

A foreseeable period! Still, for some of us (not excluding me), that's going to be pretty close. To cut a long story short – we, the spry "bestagers" from the fifties, should not get our hopes up too much. And yet, the subject is fascinating.

Let us imagine: The secret of death is a grey cube-shaped house with a pyramid roof and three hundred doors, all with a nice sign like "TELOMERE-HYPOTHESIS", "OXIDANTS-HYPOTHESIS" and "DISPOSABLE-SOMA-THEORY". No door is locked, but they all lead into their own anteroom, a dim corridor from which further doors lead off. In all the rooms, there are people, some of them whimsical figures, others serious researchers, who try to open the other doors with grotesque-looking keys to access the sacred elixir of life, the nectarine from the Zeus story. Some have already succeeded, but they only managed to get to one of the other antechambers, only to be greeted with amazement by the search team there. They decide to combine the theories of the two antechambers and celebrate them as a new step towards the great breakthrough.

That's about where we are. If one sorts out all the hypotheses concerning the causes of ageing, one arrives at two main concepts:

1. Undetermined death: after the main aim of producing offspring has been achieved, the individual decays physically and mentally.

2. Predetermined death: a death programme is inherent in the body's cells, which, for example, ends human life after 120 years at the latest.

There are countless special theories surrounding unintended death, which shed light on social, evolutionary, or whole-body aspects of this process. The argument that after the reproductive phase, there is no longer any need to maintain the life of an individual is plausible. It only continues as a result of the momentum it has. It can be prolonged by removing all the unevenness from the track - similar to the smoothing of the ice rink before the sliding curling stone. Another image would be a piece of driftwood in the stream.

These theories focus – on the molecular level – on the increasing disintegration of the body's cells with advancing age. Free radicals play a major role in this. They cause the cells to suffer from oxidation stress caused by defective oxygen atoms, which in turn are produced by the mitochondria, the "power plants of the cell". A rough idea of the importance of this process is given by the fact that several thousand DNA damages happen per day and per cell, but most of them are repaired again.

Against this idea of increasing wear and tear of the body's cells in the course of life stands the idea of a predetermined death. The idea of the expiry of the life clock is based primarily on two observations. One of them refers to the chromosomes, the command centres of the body's cells, and their tangled ends, the telomeres. With each cell division, this end shortens until no more division is possible, and the cell eventually dies. Regeneration of the telomeres is possible with the help of the enzyme *telomerase*. A very unattractive but vivid example of this are cancer cells, which could theoretically live forever if they also allowed their host organism to do so.

The second observation refers to experiments with various living organisms, e.g. the fruit fly Drosophila, the vinegar worm Caenorhabditis, or the laboratory mouse, but also simple baker's yeast. Here, the manipulation of various genes has led to a significant prolongation of life, e.g., 69 percent in a certain house mouse strain! In humans, the FOXO3-Gen is the focus of interest, which the media have already dubbed the "Methuselah gene" or the "old-age gene". A certain genotype of this gene is frequently found in people who are over 100 years old.

These theories about the ageing process – to be more precise: about the process of decline, as deterioration already begins at birth – cannot be strictly separated from each other, but overlap in part. In the overview, a confusing picture emerges, but one that is also very fascinating. You have the screws in front of you that you could turn, and you have the screwdriver in the form of genetic engineering. But now – what next?

The aforementioned guru of eternal life, Aubrey de Grey, despite all the dubiousness of his prognoses, deserves credit for putting these screws in a certain order and thus making the field of research somewhat clearer.

De Grey is a bioinformatician from Cambridge, England, and a member of many scientific committees worldwide. Incidentally, the Methuselah-Mouse-Prize, which the hapless Gustav Zehdenick desperately wants to win in the story Zeus is telling a joke, also goes back to him. De Grey postulates seven (magical!) strategies for prolonging life, which he calls SENS (Strategies for Engineered Negligible Senescence). They essentially aim at the repair of cell damage. For those interested, the article SENS Research Foundation on Wikipedia is recommended. De Grey formulates his claims quite rigorously and is accordingly controversial.

Three things should be mentioned: first, the hype in the media about life extension; second, examples of long or infinite life in the animal kingdom; and third, alternative life extension strategies.

With regard to the media hype, the following applies: The nutrition and pharmaceutical industries make good use of every new rumour about life research and propagate corresponding anti-ageing products. Creams, pills, drinks, and food refer to this or that finding (which often only consists of unsubstantiated observations), accompanied by astonishing reports of success. Reports to the contrary or relativising reports fall by the wayside. The most surprising is probably the latest report about the life-prolonging effects of red wine, which are said to be mainly based on the ingredient resveratrol, an anti-oxidant. But what about red grape juice, for example? Is it less effective? Were only the winegrowers faster than the juicers here? The industry's claims should not and cannot be soundly denied here, but scepticism seems justified. Especially those: How do the ingested substances actually reach the cells via the food tract and bloodstream, where they are supposed to perform their miraculous work? Are they perhaps broken down in the stomach and intestines and processed into something completely different? According to current knowledge, the best strategy for prolonging life is simple fasting. But how can this be sold profitably?

Animals and plants that can live for an astonishingly long time, if not forever, have been known for a long time, and the list is constantly growing. It is hoped that research into them – but also into extremely short-lived species – will provide insights into the secrets of the ageing process. It should be noted that this is always based on ideal conditions because no living creature is immune to the so-called catastrophic death, i.e., being eaten, for example. We have read about mammoth trees whose age has been proven to be up to 3000 years; we know about the simple Hydra (freshwater polyp) from the duck pond next door, several millimetres in size and eating water fleas, of which it is believed it can theoretically live indefinitely. Impressive is the equally tiny Mediterranean jellyfish Turritopsis, from whose umbrella new young jellyfish can emerge. This multicellular animal can therefore not only live indefinitely but also rejuvenate itself! That would be the next research goal after the discovery of eternal life.

Finally, a word about the classification of what has been described above seems appropriate. The continuation of "normal" biological life is not the only idea pursued under the premise of "eternal life". There are, for example, the Cryonics, who seek salvation in freezing and later thawing. Some limit themselves to their heads – "small is beautiful" also applies to eternal life. And there are the transhumanists, who want to take the evolution of the human species into their own hands and ultimately strive for a fusion of man and machine. The continuation of life as a cyborg, as a cybernetic organism. A techno-biologically optimised existence – whether as an individual being, in a swarm, or quasi as a coral colony. Or just as memory content in a folder in a computer's memory. There are no limits to the imagination (as long as imagination still exists).

These prospects may be more frightening than enticing. What seems reassuring is the hope that all this is still a long way off and will not affect us for a long time yet.

Far from it! The movement of transhumanism is developing at an impressive pace into a kind of creed and is gaining more and more followers. On a global scale, the NGO World Transhumanist Association (WTA) was already founded in 2002. It cooperates with various national groups and even specific political parties, e.g., the Transhumanists UK (former Transhumanist Party UK), the United States Transhumanist Party, and the Transhumane Partei Deutschlands (TPD). The big US-concern ALPHABET (which also holds GOOGLE) is one of the main commercial promoters of this concept. For the special purpose of life extension research, it has founded the affiliate CALICO (Californian Life Company). Given its nearly unlimited financial power and the broad industrial network which it has already established, substantial progress can be expected in the near future. Progress that is cast in the form of international patents.

So will extended life soon belong to ALPHABET? Will the entire future of mankind belong to ALPHABET? People will follow this trend, as they (almost) always do.

I have a question about this.

Imagine I am no longer seventy-six, as I am now, but one hundred and twenty years old. I am in good health, almost better than ever before. I am no longer shortsighted, my digestive problems have gone, and my right hip joint is also fine again. My diabetes and blood pressure are optimally adjusted. I could only have dreamed of my current sexual life during puberty. My brain is trimmed to top performance by a constant data connection with the cloud. All its content is also stored there. Armies of nanobots are on the move in my body to maintain it and, if necessary, repair even the smallest organic and technical ramifications. All sorts of cocktails flow into my veins from a new tank-like organ implanted in me, keeping the chemical balances constant. My mood, temperament, likes, and dislikes are balanced and constant. I know no hate and no love. I don't have to worry about what my guts tell me because I don't feel it. I also don't wonder what a thought "feels" like because I don't feel it. I don't have extreme ideas because they are deleted by the operator in advance of their creation. I do my work, and I am satisfied.

The question I spoke of is:
Is this still ME?
Or is this rather the new definition of – DEATH?

*

The above information can be easily reproduced on the internet. By entering the keywords "ageing", "biogerontology", "SENS", "CALICO", "Transhumanism" in the search engine, you will quickly find what you are looking for. A relatively clear and coherent picture emerges. One should also take note of the warning statements, e.g., by the famous physicist Stephen Hawking (†) and Microsoft co-founder Bill Gates, which can also be found on the net.

Acknowledgement

These four stories are solely a product of my fantasy. They were originally written in German. I am very happy that Elizabeth, an English native speaker and good friend of mine, helped me translate them into English. I wish to thank her for her precious contributions. Still, there might be several unusual or inappropriate wordings, mainly because the last correction was my responsibility. But I hope reading the stories is still fun. And that you, unlike me, might live forever...

For further information about the
author
and his publications
visit

http://peter-w-richter.com

https://www.youtube.com/channel/
UCcVrnfPN4o60pV-0H8UXPIg